Uncertain World

The EMP Survivor Series – Book 2

By Chris Pike

Uncertain World
The EMP Survivor Series
by Chris Pike

Edited by Felicia A. Sullivan
Formatted by Kody Boye
Cover art by Hristo Kovatliev

Dedication

To my readers: Thank you. This story would not have been possible without you and your encouragement. Y'all are the best! And to my family who has put up with all my crazy ideas and work-shopping sessions, y'all are the best too.

- *Chris*

"He conquers who endures."

- *Persius*

Foreword

So, what kind of story is this?

We have the story of an EMP unleashed on the United States, extinguishing the modern ways of society heralded by a brilliant flash of light.

Some would say it was as tantalizing as if they were gazing upon the northern lights. A mesmerizing phenomena, capturing the timeless beauty of the world. Its oceans and skies, deserts and verdant forests, great civilizations of glittering skyscrapers lit by man's invention. Of magnificent sports arenas and luxurious ocean liners, of the busy hum of life on a downtown street: food vendors, cabs, cars, rail, traffic lights, buses.

In a flash of light, it ceased.

Poof.

There were no more cell phones, instant messaging, or lazy afternoons channel surfing. No more information at the tap of a few keystrokes, or medicine, or communication, Bluetooth, apps, texts, fresh water, sanitation, rush hour traffic, radio stations, CDs, light at the flip of a switch, airplanes, drones, or anything connected to the modern world.

This is a story of a man who lived his life according to the way society said he should: get a job, marry, have children, and live happily ever after. And he *would* have lived happily ever after except for the unexpected death of his wife and a flash of light that forever would change the world.

Dillon Stockdale had thrown himself into his work, fighting bad guys as an assistant District Attorney during long days at the local courthouse. He was supposed to have retired and grown old with his wife, have grandkids he bounced on his knee, entertaining them with spooky ghost stories. However, it wasn't meant to be. His wife died suddenly, derailing his carefully planned life. He immersed his grief in work, meaningful work, or so he told himself, because at work he was able to escape the bleak loneliness of their house, a landscape as barren as the moon.

He was a man strong of mind and body, a no nonsense man who couldn't be bothered with small talk and cocktail parties, shiny loafers and bowties, and casual laughter, because under the façade of a civilized man lay a man sizzling for change.

We also have a woman, Holly Hudson. As lonely as Dillon Stockdale, yet who on the surface she 'had it all,' being considered successful by society's standards. She was his formidable adversary in the courtroom, known to be unflappable and one who won impossible cases, a worthy foe by any standard.

From her perfectly coiffed hair and silk suits, it was impossible to break Holly's porcelain veneer. But like any fine china, the tiniest crack or chip could undermine the integrity of a structure, collapsing it into unrepairable fragments. Yet from the broken pieces picked up and reassembled, something new came.

Something better.

One day during a brief moment before the EMP struck, when it was quiet in the courtroom, Holly had snuck a peek at Dillon, admiring the way he carried himself and the confidence he exuded. Confused and embarrassed, she immediately distracted herself by perusing a legal brief, yet her interest had been piqued.

Soon after, a crack appeared and widened into a dark chasm at the realization she had never baked cookies for a Cub Scout meeting, or tucked a child into bed, or dried tears from a scraped knee, all because she was afraid to live, or to feel regret, or to lose someone she loved.

She had indeed suffered a tremendous loss at a tender age, and had felt it ever since in the molecules of her soul.

She had found meaning in her life by throwing herself into work (or so she told herself), poring over legal briefs and case files and researching obscure laws that had only garnered a slide in a law school lecture, all to win a case. Her determination made her a formidable opponent in the courtroom and won her not only cases, but the admiration of fellow colleagues.

We also have Cassie, Dillon's daughter, who has forged her own way in modern society, belonging to the generation who grew up in the internet age. Like her father, she is tenacious and perseveres. She's smart and will rely on all her wits to survive in this new world.

Ryan Manning, a young man who befriended Cassie on the ill-fated flight that crash landed in the swamps of Louisiana, has entered a new life as well. Together, they survived and gradually learned to trust each other, divulging their hopes and dreams of lives interrupted.

Battles will be won in hand to hand combat instead of keystrokes on a keyboard, or sending a drone to do the dirty work, or the input of a few coordinated numbers, or the push of a metaphorical red button.

Indeed, the new way of life will require each of them to walk the maze of unseen dangers encountered in places they thought were safe.

Chapter 1

"Don't make any sudden moves and nobody gets hurt."

Ryan Manning, Cassie Stockdale, and James Morley, survivors of a plane that crash landed into the Louisiana backcountry had been walking for several days when they made camp under a massive Virginia oak on a dry patch of land.

The trek across unfamiliar terrain had been more taxing than they could have imagined. That, and the fact they weren't prepared for a hike, had made matters worse.

Weary and hungry, they made a fire to warm their hands. Too tired to get up during the night to add more kindling, the fire had withered to coals.

Cassie lay shivering under the thin gray airplane blanket, her cold toes poking out of the frayed ends. Her tennis shoes and socks had gotten soaked the day before so she had put them by the fire to dry out.

Long fingers of the morning sun threaded through the trees and onto the land. The grass was wet with shimmering dew; the morning air still cold from the night.

Cassie had been awake for a few minutes, listening to the morning awakening with the sounds of the woods, dismissing the crackling of twigs breaking as an animal scurrying in the brush. When she heard that ominous command, a burst of adrenaline flooded her body. It wasn't exactly the kind of alarm clock she had hoped for. Her heart hammered against her chest and she lay as still as she could. Maybe whoever it was would take what they needed and leave. She opened an eye a slit taking in her surroundings.

She was on her side, facing the withering coals. James was sleeping on the other side of the dying campfire. He was snoring and had his back to her.

Great.

He wouldn't be any help.

Earlier, Ryan told Cassie nature was calling and he had to go do his business. "I'll only be gone a few minutes," he'd said.

A terrified thought crossed Cassie's mind. Suppose whoever had said *Don't make any sudden moves and nobody gets hurt* had already hurt Ryan, or worse, killed him.

Cassie held her breath, afraid to move.

"I know you're awake, little lady, so you can get up. Be quiet and don't make any fast moves. And keep your hands where I can see them."

The man shouldered a weathered old Winchester model 12 pump action shotgun. He racked the handguard to chamber a round to show he meant what he said.

Cassie took a quick glance at the guy. "Don't shoot," she pleaded.

"Do as I say and nobody gets hurt."

Cassie estimated the man was about fifty, his clothes worn yet clean. And though he was built like an ox with wide, muscled shoulders, his skin weathered from the sun, he didn't appear as menacing as his warning words were. There was something kind about his face, although Cassie couldn't quite put her finger on it. Cassie's heart skipped a beat when he leveled the shotgun, pointing it directly at her.

"What do you want?" the man asked.

"I'm wondering the same thing about you," Cassie replied.

"I ask the questions, not you. What are you doing here?"

"Nothing."

"Wrong answer," he shot back. "Try again."

"Camping for the night," Cassie said, hoping the waver in her voice wasn't noticeable. She smiled, but with apprehension. "We're trying to get home."

"Where's home?" the man asked.

"Houston."

The man doubled over and let out a belly laugh so loud it spooked a flock of sparrows perched in a nearby tree. "Houston! You're walking home to Houston? From *here*! I've never heard of anything so ridiculous."

Hearing the commotion, James woke, rolled over, and asked, "What's going on here? Who are you?"

"Name's Garrett," the tall man's voice boomed. "And you?" he asked, motioning with the shotgun.

"Whoa," James said. His hands went up in the air, indicating he wasn't a threat to the man. His eyes zeroed in on the deadly end of the shotgun. "We don't want any trouble. I'm trying to get home too."

"To Houston like your lady friend is?"

"Austin, actually," James said.

"This keeps getting better and better, don't it? Y'all on some kind of reality TV show or something?"

"All the camera men and production crew went home for the night to their five star hotel, complete with room service," Cassie deadpanned. Her earlier smile had evaporated into an impatient frown.

"*Naked and Afraid* meets Bear Grylls," Garrett said, "but without the naked part?"

"I'm joking," Cassie said.

"Me too," Garrett replied.

Rising, James brushed off his pants and said, "I'm James Morley. This is Cassie Stockdale."

At hearing the name 'Stockdale' Garrett lowered his shotgun and swiveled his attention to Cassie. "Stockdale, huh?"

"Yes," Cassie replied weakly.

"You any relation to Dillon Stockdale?"

"Why?" Cassie asked. Her eyes flicked to James, hoping he would give her some type of instruction on what to say.

James shrugged.

"You his daughter?" Garrett asked.

Cassie took a long moment about how to answer, knowing that

people didn't like district attorneys because maybe a relative of theirs had been prosecuted and put away for a long time. Taking a gamble this Garrett guy wasn't one of them, she rose, stood straight, and announced proudly, "I am."

Garrett ran a hand across the stubble on his chin. "I thought I saw a faint resemblance."

"Do you know my dad?" Cassie was instantly relieved they had found a friendly face. She was also intrigued that someone of his backwoods appearance would be familiar with a big city prosecutor from the next state.

"Not personally, but I know he was prosecuting Cole Cassel. That son of a bitch," Garrett said. He kicked the toe of his boot in the dirt, loosening a rock embedded in the fertile Atchafalaya Basin soil. "Been reading about the trial in the Houston paper. Seen your daddy's picture in the paper. I get it specially delivered to my property twice a week. It's a little late, but it's still news. I like to keep up with current events, even if I do live way out in the boondocks. Funny thing, though, I haven't had any mail delivery at all this week."

"Why are you following the trial?" Cassie asked, interested in this new revelation.

"That bastard Cassel killed my son in NOLA. Left his wife to raise my grandson without his father." Garrett looked away and cleared his throat. "My son was in the wrong place at the wrong time. He was gettin' milk and bread at a convenience store late one evenin' when a turf war broke out between Cassel and a rival gang member. My son was an innocent bystander."

Garrett explained the rest of the story that a crooked district attorney, who had since been disbarred because of kickbacks, failed to introduce evidence at the trial that would have successfully convicted Cole. "The trial was a sham from the beginning."

"I'm sorry about your son," Cassie said. "Cole's a bad man, but my dad is smart and honest and will see to it he goes to jail for a long, long time. I talked to my dad a few days ago and he said he thought he was about to win the trial. If he can't get justice for your son, then it will be for somebody else. The penalty will be the same."

"Let's hope so," Garrett said. "So tell me what y'all are doing here." His eyes swept over the camp. "And where's your camping equipment? I've never seen such a poor camp. With that and the fact you're on private property, you're lucky I didn't shoot you. I've had a problem with poachers lately. A game warden was killed last year, and they never caught the murderous SOB." Glancing at James, still wearing scuffed oxford shoes, Garrett added, "And who camps in a suit?"

"I didn't have a choice," James said gruffly. "If I had known I was going to have to walk home I would have dressed accordingly." He glanced at his shoes. "And I would have worn boots instead of oxfords because my feet hurt." He removed a shoe and massaged his foot.

"Got a point there," Garrett said.

Cassie interrupted. "You won't believe this…"

"Try me," Garrett said.

"We survived a plane crash, and when nobody came for us, we walked out of there."

"Really?" Garrett said incredulously. "Some sort of prop plane or something?"

"No," Cassie said. "A 737 with about a hundred people on the plane."

"That's no good. Where'd the plane crash? And where's everybody else?"

"We're it."

"What do you mean by that?"

"Everybody else is dead," Cassie said. The words hung in the air while Garrett digested the revelation. "Me, James, and…" Cassie trailed off, diverting her eyes to the ground. "I don't know where the plane crashed. I'm guessing somewhere southeast of here. The land all looks the same. We're lost."

"I can believe that. Good thing I found you 'cause you are in the middle of acres and acres of swampy woods. You could have died out here."

Cassie and James agreed.

"How long have you been walking?" Garrett asked.

"Several days," Cassie said. "Do you have anything? Water or food you could give us? I can repay you once I get home."

"That won't be necessary. The enemy of my enemy is my friend. And as of now, Cassie Stockdale, you're my friend. I'll get you something to eat at my house," Garrett said, hitching his chin in the direction where the house was. "It's no Hilton, so if you're expecting anything fancy, you'll be disappointed."

"We will be extremely grateful for whatever you have."

"Just you and uh…" Garrett said, snapping his fingers.

"James Morley," James said, the irritation is his voice mounting.

"Only you and James?"

Cassie snuck a peek at James, hoping he would help her make a decision regarding her decision to keep Ryan's presence a secret. She wanted to believe Garrett was a decent guy, but still wasn't convinced one hundred percent. If anything happened out here, nobody knew where they were.

The unmistakable sound of a shotgun being racked caught their attention, and it wasn't Garrett doing the racking.

Chapter 2

"Don't anyone move," a surly male voice said. "I've got a loaded shotgun that can take out two of you with one blast."

To say Garrett was utterly surprised was an understatement. His mind did a quick search for voice recognition, but he failed to match the voice with a face. It had a Cajun inflection to it, not so much southern, but the sound of someone who had lived in the swamp all his life. Garrett did as told and didn't even blink. He was breathing slow and steady, keeping attuned to the voice coming from behind him.

Cassie's heart skipped a beat and her eyes flicked to James. She crouched down.

"You, big man, the one with the Winchester," the unknown man said, this time more menacing, "drop your shotgun. And if you try anything funny, I'll blow a hole in you and you'll be dead before you hit the ground."

Garrett reluctantly lowered the shotgun to the ground.

"Well now," the man said, walking over to where he could easily see the three. He zeroed in on Cassie. "Stand up," he ordered.

Cassie didn't move. She kept her eyes downcast while she quickly searched the campsite for anything she could use as a weapon. Her eyes went to the rocks circling the campfire.

"Don't get any ideas like picking up one of those rocks."

Cassie swallowed hard.

"Stand up!"

Cassie eased up from the ground and stood as instructed. Her shoulders were rolled forward and she was becoming more concerned for her safety. She sensed the man was eyeing her over.

"Turn around," the man barked. "And you, big man, don't move a muscle unless I tell you to. Understand?"

Garrett nodded.

"Kick the shotgun over here to me."

Garrett glared at the man then reluctantly kicked the shotgun in the man's direction. He balled his fists in frustration.

"That's more like it." He sidled up to Cassie and inspected her as if she was a horse, touching her hair, running his fingers down her arms and back. "A little on the skinny side, but you'll fetch a good price."

Cassie furrowed her brow, not quite understanding what he meant by that statement until the realization sunk in. "I'm not going anywhere with you. I'll die first." Her lips were tight and her voice was steadfast.

The man took a fast step toward her and roughly grabbed her hair, forcing her head back. He wet his lips. His face was inches away from her and his breath hot. "I can arrange that too, so you'd better—"

With the precision of a laser, a rock struck the back of the man's head and made a cracking thud when it popped his skull.

The shock of the bone-crunching hit dazed the man for a moment and he released his grip on Cassie.

Cassie heaved her knee with all her might and struck him in the soft flesh of his groin.

The man grunted and bent over at the waist.

Cassie took an unsure step back, her eyes widening with fear, watching in horror.

The man brought up the shotgun, leveling it at her.

In the second that Cassie had kneed the guy, Garrett sprang up and lunged, throwing his body on the ground, arms stretched out, reaching for his shotgun.

Cassie stood there as if she was petrified wood. Her eyes were big with fear and she willed her body to move but her legs were frozen. Unable to move, she steeled herself for what was sure to follow.

When the shotgun blast sounded, Cassie flinched and closed her eyes. Bending at the waist, she hunched over and instinctively covered her head with both hands.

There was another shotgun blast and the man that had threatened her with a fate worse than death crumpled to the ground, face down. There was a gaping hole the size of a plate in his back and another one on his side.

Blood oozed onto the ground.

Ryan was standing at the edge of the clearing, his eyes focused like lasers on Garrett. His pitching arm was poised high to hurl another skull-cracking rock and if Garrett made any intimidating moves, Ryan planned to show him the strength of his previously ninety mph throwing arm.

Cassie bolted to Ryan, burying her face in his chest. The brutality of seeing a man shot to death in real life was nothing like it was on TV, where the reality of death was sanitized with camera angles and makeup that could be washed off.

Ryan put his arms around Cassie holding her. She trembled uncontrollably. He patted her back. "It's okay. Are you hurt?"

Cassie mumbled weakly.

"Good. You're safe now. Everything will be okay."

Garrett stood tall and asked, "Who are you?"

"My name is Ryan."

A large hound dog came limping into camp, holding a paw up and toddling on three legs. He hobbled over to Garrett, much to Ryan's astonishment.

"What's going on?" Ryan asked. He cast a confused glance at Garrett and the dog.

"This sorry SOB was about to send us all to an early grave, and Cassie, well, he had other plans for her." Garrett came up to Cassie. "You didn't say you had a third person with you," he said, somewhat annoyed.

Cassie didn't answer.

Garrett faced Ryan. "Nice throw. You saved our hides."

"Thanks. I was a pitcher in high school. Never knew baseball would save lives."

"I could throw a mean fast ball in my time," Garrett said. "Obviously you did too."

Ryan sized Garrett up. He was tall, barrel-chested, with arms that could easily swing an ax, and if the guy had lived up north, he would have fit in with the lumberjack crowd.

"A mean fast ball works every time," Ryan said.

Garrett took a step toward the dead guy and poked him with the end of his shotgun. Satisfied there was no movement, he heaved the dead man over on his back and studied him, trying to determine if he knew him. Garrett ran a hand through his salt and pepper hair, thinking.

"You recognize him?" Ryan asked.

"Nope. I'm guessing he was a poacher. I had just told your friends we've had trouble with poachers, but I never figured they were into human trafficking." He addressed Cassie, who had calmed down from the excitement. "Be careful out here. You never know who is good and who isn't."

"I'll be careful," Cassie said, chewing on a ragged nail. "Sorry about not telling you we had a third person. I didn't know if you meant to harm us."

"Yeah, well, I'll let it pass because your friend found my dog." Garrett set his shotgun down and kneeled on the hard ground. "Come here, boy. Come here."

The dog didn't move.

"What's wrong, boy?" Garrett asked, worried there was something wrong with his dog. He glared at Ryan. "What did you do to my dog?"

"Nothing," Ryan said. "He's having trouble walking. I found him curled under a tree, and when I went to him, he didn't run, so I figured he was injured."

Garrett grunted and gave his dog a good once over, letting his hands fly over him, checking for injuries. He was covered in mud and had stickers in his coat. Garrett took each of the dog's paws in his hand and with the skill of a surgeon, he inspected each pad. He found several one inch thorns wedged in between two of the pads on each front paw. When Garrett pulled out the embedded thorns stuck deep in the dog's skin, the dog pulled back his paws and yelped.

Ryan, Cassie, and James stood with their mouths agape, awed at the tenderness the ox of a man showed his dog.

Garrett put his hands under the dog's belly and helped him up. "There. That feels better don't it?" Garrett asked in a warm and soothing voice. He stroked the dog's head.

The dog thumped his tail.

"Thank you for finding my dog. I don't think he could have made it home in the shape he was in. I've been worried sick about him. He's been gone for three nights, and I could hear him baying at some varmint, probably a coon. When he didn't come home I knew something was wrong. It would have killed me not to know what had happened." Garrett stood and extended his hand to Ryan. "This was my son's dog."

Ryan shook hands with Garrett. "Glad I could be of help. I'm Ryan Manning, in case you didn't get it the first time around."

"Nice to get a proper introduction. Let's get you folks back to my house. Too much excitement for one morning, and you look like you could eat a good breakfast," he said, eyeing each of them, noting their dirty clothes, "and a long bath. Water's not hot, seeing as we don't have any electricity, but it will get you just as clean." Garrett picked up his shotgun and also the dead guy's shotgun. "No need to let that go to waste."

Cassie glanced back upon the dead man. "What are you going to do about him?"

"The guy that was about to kill us? And the one who would have sold you to the highest bidder?"

Cassie nodded.

"Let him rot."

Chapter 3

Ten minutes later after a hike through tangled trees lining a bayou, lowland clearings, and more trees, they came to a dirt road which led them to Garrett's house.

The wood frame house was situated on a two acre clearing with an orchard of fig, pear, persimmon, and loquat trees. A mayhaw bush that had been cultivated from the swamp rounded out the orchard. A garden teemed with seasonal vegetables.

Thick woods surrounded the property. The yard had been recently mowed and when they came up to the house, a young boy happily bounded down the steps and ran toward them.

Garrett held out his arms and waited for the little boy to smash into him. Garrett scooped up the boy, swung him high in the air, and planted him on his hip.

The big dog sauntered over to Garrett, tongue hanging out and wiggling in excitement.

"Grandpa, you found Gumbo!" The child's voice was filled with innocent joy.

"Actually, this nice man over here found him." Garrett swung his grandson down to the ground. "This is my grandson, Skeeter," he said, ruffling the top of the boy's crew cut. Skeeter made a face and shooed away Garrett's hand. "Skeeter, say 'hi' to these nice folks."

Skeeter, about five years old, shied away behind his grandpa and peeked out from around him. He spied the ragged bunch with curiosity. "Who are these people, Grandpa?"

"These folks are tryin' to get home to Houston. They've got a long walk in front of them and they're hungry."

"Where's Youston?" Skeeter asked, trying out the new word.

"A long way from here. Go on in and tell your mama to make a mess of biscuits and gravy. Scrambled eggs too. Tell her to set out some of the dewberry preserves and butter if we still have any. Everyone needs a little fat on their bodies. And be sure to feed Gumbo!" Garrett sent the boy on his way with a loving pat on his rump.

"Okay, Grandpa," Skeeter said. He bolted to the house, yelling for his mama.

Garrett explained that his daughter-in-law's folks couldn't afford to feed two more mouths, so they turned her and Skeeter away. Garrett was happy to take them in and told them they could live with him as long as they wanted to.

"Family has to stick together. I live my life according to the three Fs: faith, family, and firearms," he said, patting his shotgun. "Remember that and you'll always be okay."

Cassie nodded and repeated the words. "Faith, family, and firearms. I like that. I'll remember it."

"You folks want to clean up or eat first?" Garrett asked.

Three voices said in unison, "Eat first."

Cassie walked into the house, followed by Gumbo, who trotted over to his food bowl and gulped down the food in it. She wiped her shoes on the mat inside the front door, and was immediately struck by how neat and homey the house was. A wood-burning stove sat in the middle of the house, dividing the living area from the kitchen. The wood floor was covered with throw rugs, and the sofa had a homemade colorful quilt draped over it. There were a couple of lamps on the end tables. The cozy eat-in kitchen had all the modern appliances with a refrigerator, oven, and cooktop. A microwave sat on a stand. Cassie noticed a table and four chairs with vinyl coverings that were definitely a throwback to the sixties. The bookshelves in the living area caught her eye and she went over to check out the books.

"Hello," a female voice called out. "I hear y'all are hungry. I'm Adelaide, and that's my boy Skeeter. I have to apologize because the electricity is out. It'll take me a little bit longer to get the grill fired up and breakfast ready for you folks. If I had known we were going to have company I would have already had something prepared." She eyed the rangy bunch.

"Thank you so much," Cassie said. "We got lost and your father-in-law found us."

Adelaide nodded like it was no big deal.

After introducing herself, Ryan, and James, Cassie asked, "Can I help you with anything?"

"Actually, yes. You and Skeeter can come with me and we'll check the henhouse for eggs. I had some store bought ones in the refrigerator, but we ate those the day after the electricity went off. It's strange, we've never had the electricity stay off for this long unless there's a hurricane or a tropical storm. It doesn't matter," she said waving a hand, "we've got plenty of food to get us through. We'll let the menfolk talk a while." Adelaide washed her hands and wiped them on a hand towel. "Garrett, breakfast will be ready in a little while."

"Thanks, let me know if I can do anything," he said.

Garrett motioned for Ryan and James to sit at the table with him. He poured each a steaming cup of coffee from a thermos, explaining he had boiled water early in the morning. "Watch out for the grinds," he said.

"At this point," James said, "I'm so hungry and thirsty I'd drink grinds and all."

"So," Garrett said, taking a seat, "tell me about the plane crash."

James and Ryan told Garrett about what they remembered, and what they experienced regarding the sudden loss of power.

"It was deathly quiet," Ryan said, "and I guess I must have passed out for a while. I remember waking up and wondering if I was alive or dead."

"Me too," James said. "When I came to, I had no idea where I was or what had happened. I remember Cassie screaming when I grabbed her ankle."

"Believe me," Cassie said, poking her head around a corner, "you gave me the shock of my life."

"We tried using our cell phones but they wouldn't work," Ryan added. "We thought at first there was no cell tower nearby, but we couldn't even get our phones to turn on."

"Interesting," Garrett said. He mulled over the events and the lack of cell service. Garrett didn't have a cell phone but he said he had seen plenty of other people use them on the country road. "There's a tower not far from here so I don't know why the cell phones wouldn't be working."

"We waited for help but when we didn't see any search planes," Ryan said, "we knew it was time to save ourselves."

"That's what I would have done. It's always best to be self-sufficient. I admire your tenacity," Garrett said.

"After breakfast, do you think you could drive us into town?" Ryan asked.

"I would if I could, but my truck won't start," Garrett said. "I figured it was the battery, but the engine wouldn't even make a sound. I tried using my phone—"

"What kind of phone do you have?" Ryan interrupted.

"An old fashioned landline over there," Garrett said, pointing to an antique stand by the sofa.

Rising from the chair, Ryan said, "Mind if I make a call?"

"You can try," Garrett said. "There's something wrong with it though. The phone only works half the time. Now that I think about it, I started having problems with it the same day the electricity went off. I've been able to make a couple of local calls, but only to people with a landline. Cell numbers aren't working."

"Hmm," Ryan said. He subconsciously scratched the side of his head, mulling over the events of the past several days.

"What do you think is going on?" Garrett asked. He took a sip of coffee then leaned into the table. "Electricity, phones, cars—they all stopped working at the same time."

Ryan frowned. "I have an idea and it's not good."

Chapter 4

Cole Cassel sat in the former sheriff's office contemplating his next move. Taking over the office had been easier than he'd expected, and he was feeling mighty important about now.

Driving into town in the ancient pickup he had stolen, one which the EMP hadn't affected, Cole came upon the lone sheriff on a rarely traveled road. The sheriff had been on his way to make a courtesy call on a landowner who wasn't answering his phone when the cruiser died.

The sheriff had spent a couple of nights in his cruiser waiting for help or for someone to drive by. The lack of activity was worrisome and he had made a decision to walk the twenty miles back to town when luck would have it, he saw an approaching truck. Finally, he'd get help.

Since he wasn't one to miss a good opportunity, Cole did the neighborly thing, which was to stop and help. He also did an uncivilized thing, which was to shoot the sheriff in the back.

Cole stripped the sheriff of anything useful, including his badge and service pistol. He considered taking the pants then decided against it after he saw the amount of blood and guts staining the fabric. Cole had his standards, low though they may be, and wearing bloodstained clothes was not on the short list.

Picking up the sheriff's 10 gallon hat, Cole tried it on for good measure. It fit well enough. He dragged the corpse to the roadside, rolled the body into the ditch, and covered it with a few sticks. The wild hogs and coyotes would clean up the rest.

Rummaging around in the trunk, Cole found a Remington model 870 pump action shotgun with an eighteen inch barrel. It held six rounds in the magazine plus one in the chamber.

Christmas came early for Cole, because he also found two boxes of ammo for the shotgun. Picking up one of the twenty-five round boxes, Cole mentally patted himself on the back. It was exactly what he needed.

He hopped in his truck and checked his appearance in the review mirror. He practiced tipping his hat as if he was a swashbuckling westerner passing by a damsel twirling a parasol who demurely eyed him over.

Not too shabby, he thought. Especially with a shiny badge. He had always wanted one of those, and now that he had one, he displayed it for everyone to see. He pinned the badge on his hat.

He was the law now.

Driving to the sheriff's office in the rural town, Cole passed places which brought back long repressed memories, especially from high school. A wave of nostalgia hit him when he recalled the last football game he played. The people cheering him, high-fiving him, the adoring accolades the coaches bestowed on him. Then there was Holly, a freckle-faced seventeen year old.

The years and his lifestyle may have hardened Cole, but he didn't let that get in his way of remembering Holly. She had always been too good for him, seeing that he was from the wrong side of the tracks.

In a brief moment of clarity, Cole realized he had screwed up royally, though the moment didn't last long.

He could have never lived up to her standards.

And that kid she had? At the time Cole was too immature to admit the kid could be his and there was no way he was going to fork over child support. The years went by and the resemblance couldn't be dismissed. Some unexplainable curiosity to keep up with the kid had consumed Cole and he had made it a point to make people let him know what was going on. He had pictures sent to him on the kid's birthday, even knew what schools the kid attended.

Although he had blackmailed some of his small-town informants, others he paid off.

There were whispers about the kid's real parents, and when the kid got old enough to understand, the adoptive parents whisked him away to a far corner of Texas.

Cole had eyes there too.

The kid was now grown, and Cole had made it a point to get within arm's length of the kid one day in the French Quarter in New Orleans. However, when push came to shove, Cole chickened out and walked away. He had forked over a lot of Benjamins to his network of spies to keep tabs on the kid, making sure he was safe. Cole wasn't going to let anything happen to the kid.

He had convinced Holly to take the case for trial. She had fallen for the threat hook, line, and sinker. If she had lost the case, Cole wouldn't have followed through with his death threat, because he considered anyone who killed their offspring to be on the same level as child molesters.

The last time Cole saw the kid, a brief moment of pride captured him. He had the same long legs and wide shoulders as Cole, maybe not as tall, though, which he guessed came from Holly's side. He had dark hair, which was thought to come from American Indian ancestry, according to family lore on Cole's father's side.

Cole knew there was an old couple in town who had pledged to the kid's parents that if he was ever in trouble, the kid could count on them. The elderly couple, who kept mostly to themselves, had at one time been close friends with the kid's adoptive parents.

The old man spent his time puttering around in the garage and doing yard work, while the old woman whiled away the time crocheting. The kid had never been back to the town of his birth after being whisked away to West Texas. It was just as well. Better to let sleeping dogs lie.

Taking his feet off of the desk, Cole went over to the window and peered outside, recalling how easy it had been to take over the sheriff's office.

Two of the deputies had put up a feeble attempt to protect the integrity of the station, but after seeing Cole assassinate a deputy he had captured, they immediately gave up their arms and swore allegiance to Cole.

Peace officers in rural America weren't used to the brutal methods Cole was willing to implement to take over and control the town. Cole had come into town like he knew the place, the people, and what they would or wouldn't do.

He found deputies Jed and Cleve in a back office where they had barricaded themselves. Without the use of a radio or phone, they had been helpless to call for reinforcements.

He had told the deputies to give up or he would kill the secretary and her daughter, who had come to the office to deliver cookies they had baked using a generator to power their oven.

The mother had pleaded with Cole not to hurt her daughter, Kelsey, a pretty nineteen year old who went to the local community college in the next town. The pleas fell on deaf and uncaring ears.

"You have to the count of three!" Cole yelled to the deputies. He was standing on the other side of the door, holding the barrel of the Glock to the older woman's temple.

"Please you don't have to do this," she begged. "I can give you whatever you want."

"Shut up," he said. "You don't have anything I want. One! Two!" he yelled to the deputies in the locked office. "Three!"

There was the loud and sickening sound of a bullet obliterating the skull of Kelsey's mother, and the thud of her lifeless body hitting the floor.

"Kelsey's next!" Cole shouted. He roughly grabbed Kelsey by the arm. "You'd better come out with your hands where I can see them."

"One, two—"

"We're coming out!" one of the deputies said. "Don't shoot!"

The deputies were dressed in their khaki uniforms complete with an ammo belt, baton, flashlight, and a now useless radio. Cole motioned for them to hand over their Glocks and extra ammo.

Kelsey had crumpled to the floor next to her dead mother. Jed took a step to console her.

"Did I say you could move?" Cole barked.

Jed stopped in his tracks. "You killed her mother."

"No shit, Sherlock," Cole said. He walked over to a desk, pushed off some papers, and sat down. He took the lid off the Tupperware container full of cookies and picked out the biggest one.

"Homemade?"

No one responded.

"Are you people deaf?" Cole asked.

Still no answer.

"I said," Cole raised his voice, "are these cookies homemade?"

Jed stole a peek at Cleve, who didn't have a clue what to do or how to help. This was something Jed hadn't counted on, not in a sleepy little town like this. He was only six months on the job, barely qualifying to be a deputy in the sheriff's office after a string of unsatisfying and low-paying jobs. He was no hero, but he liked the feeling of authority when he put on his uniform. In fact, he stood taller. Plus the ladies that hadn't bothered to notice him before did so now.

He was one to know where his bread was buttered and if this guy was the new butter churner, well, so be it. Jed would be the first to ask how much cream was needed.

After a long silence, Kelsey squeaked, "Yes, they're homemade."

Cole took a bite. "Chocolate chip. I like 'em. You're a good cook. You can live."

Kelsey brought her knees up to her chin, wrapped her arms around her legs, and hung her head.

"You," he said to Jed, "go get me a glass of water. Cookies make me thirsty."

"On it," Jed said.

Taking the glass of water Jed handed him, Cole gulped it down. "Kelsey, you can run along home now."

Afraid to move, Kelsey peeked out over her folded arms, her eyes bouncing from Cole to Jed and Cleve.

"Boo!" Cole said.

Kelsey shot up and bolted out of the room. She ran out the front doors without looking back.

"Make sure she doesn't come back," Cole said.

"What do you want us to do?" Cleve asked.

"I'm sure you can think of something." Cole wiped cookie crumbs from his chin. "We need to have a talk because I'm running the show now. You boys may not know it, but I'm from here, even went to high school here. I plan to make this my town and this here's your chance to get in on the ground floor."

"How do you plan to accomplish that?" Jed asked, his interest piqued.

"Good question," Cole said. "I may keep you also."

For the next half hour, Cole outlined his plan of closing the borders of the county by not letting in any outsiders unless they paid a toll. He'd need a posse of about ten men who weren't squeamish about killing or carrying out orders. "You think we could round up men like that?"

Like a teacher's pet, Jed was the first one to thrust his hand straight in the air.

Cole nodded, giving Jed permission to speak.

"I got some buddies who'd be interested, but only if there's something in it for them."

"There'll be plenty of something for them."

"Like what?"

"Anything they want. Liquor, money, cigarettes. Most of all," Cole said, lowering his voice, "they'll have power. I need two lieutenants who'll be my right hand men." Cole got up from the chair and went over to the county map on the wall. Taking a black marks-a-lot, he drew a line straight down the center. "Jed, which side do you want?"

"East side."

"What about you, Cleve? You with us, or do you want to end up like Kelsey's mother?"

It didn't take Cleve long to answer, especially seeing how quickly Jed had jumped on the bandwagon. Cole was in power now, and to do anything foolish at the moment would only get him a bullet to the head.

"You with me?" Cole asked. "I'm not asking again."

"Yes, I'm with you," Cleve said.

"Good. Now I want you boys to clean up this mess in here. I certainly have no need for dead people."

Chapter 5

Dillon, Holly, and Buster left the comfort of Henri's fish camp. Henri had packed them several days' worth of provisions including deer jerky, two loaves of homemade bread, pickled beets, and peaches. Hidden in the pack was a flask of whiskey in case they needed to take the edge off of things. And if anybody needed to take the edge off, Dillon was the person.

Henri had never seen anyone so downtrodden by life and all its challenges. He supposed the man had a right to feel the way he did because he had failed to protect his family.

Dillon had always carefully chosen which battles to fight, because in the end it wasn't winning the battle that mattered, it was winning the war.

He had failed miserably.

It was the victor who enjoyed the spoils, whether it was toasting a hard-fought win in the courtroom, or a kid dusting off dirt from a playground fight.

For Dillon, there were no toasts or sympathy 'attaboy' pats on the back reassuring him, *'there'll be another time, another chance'*. No cheering section telling him, *'it's okay, you did your best'*. No wife to go home to telling him, *'I love you'*.

His purpose in life had been to be a good husband and a good father, and didn't a good man protect his family? Provide for them? Guide them? He had been helpless to protect Amy from the aneurism and her resulting death, and no amount of modern medicine could have saved her. Watching her take her last breath after he signed papers to have life support removed had been the hardest thing he had ever done. That was, until he thought about his daughter, Cassie.

He tortured himself thinking about the last moments of her life, replaying their last conversation over and over in his mind. She would only have had minutes left to live after their conversation. Damn whoever caused the EMP.

He only had his memories of failing and self-doubt about the choices he had made because he had lost what mattered to him most in life.

There had been numerous obstacles to overcome in his journey to find Cassie. Number one on the list had been Holly. If she hadn't been injured…if he hadn't taken her in…hadn't, well, if he hadn't fallen for her, maybe he could have found his daughter, or at least found her body.

If what the plane crash survivor had told Henri was true, her body could have fallen anywhere within a hundred miles of the crash site.

The horses plodded on, the pastures and trees segueing seamlessly from swampy land to woodland as Holly and Dillon journeyed to Holly's ranch.

Wind brushed the horses and the steady rhythm of their gait lulled Dillon back to Henri's house, to where he had recovered. He mentally replayed what Henri had said about the second survivor he had seen.

"This old boy came straggling in, barely alive. I was sittin' on my porch here smokin' a see-gar like I am now," Henri had said, taking a puff. "I saw what I thought was a lost goat. Whoowhee!" Henri exclaimed, slapping his knee. "He was crawlin' on all fours and was all beat up, clothes hangin' in tatters, knees bloodied. I've never seen me a man in such bad shape."

"What did he have to say?" Dillon had asked.

"He said he was on a plane that lost power. Somethin' about the engines up and died, all of them at the same time."

"It could have been any plane," Dillon said.

"But it wasn't," Henri said solemnly. "The man could barely talk, him being so thirsty and all. I gave him a drink of water." Henri glanced at Dillon. "You was still out like a light the whole time. It was Hollyberry who helped me."

"You mean Holly."

"Yes, sir. Hollyberry. You ever seen a holly tree?"

"I'm not sure," Dillon said.

"They're beautiful and hardy, like your Holly. But if you don't handle them correctly, you'll get pricked by spiky thorns. Nurture them and they'll protect you, give you shade when you need it, protect you from cold and heat. Predators too. Like what your Holly did…killing that alligator who surely would'a had you for dinner, then let whatever was left of you to rot in the swamp." Henri took another puff of the cigar. "You seem like a good man, Dillon, who's worthy of a good woman. Holly's one fine woman. Remember that."

"I will. Tell me the rest of the story."

"Holly helped me drag the man inside and we gave him water and food and let him rest. When he came to, he told us about surviving a plane crash. He said he was from Houston and was flying to Atlanta by way of NOLA. When he told her that Holly got all excited." Henri took a puff of the cigar and blew out a smoke ring. "Apparently the man and your daughter were on the same flight. Holly showed him a picture of your daughter—the one you had in your wallet—and that's when he got real sad. He said she was sittin' two rows in front of him and he had even helped her with the overhead, overhead…" Henri searched for the right word.

"Bin."

"Yes, overhead bin. He said she was real pretty and nice, and when he heard her name—"

"Calista."

Henri's gaze dropped to the ground. "I'm sorry about your daughter."

"Thank you."

"He said the only reason he remembered her name was because he has a daughter named Calista." After a beat, Henri said, "It's a beautiful name, just like she must have been. You want me to go on?"

"Was she with anyone?"

"He didn't say. The plane was full and busy with all sorts of people. He said he remembered the plane coming apart and the seat your daughter was in was sucked out of the plane."

"Did he say how high the plane was? Or how fast it was going? If he didn't see her actually die, there could still be hope."

"Nobody can survive being sucked out of a plane."

Dillon reluctantly nodded.

"We didn't ask him much more, he was too traumatized. He slept for fifteen straight hours and after that he said he had to get home to his wife and family."

That was what Henri had told Dillon several days prior. Dillon surmised it would have been foolish to keep searching for Cassie after his near brush with death. Besides, he still didn't feel one hundred percent, especially after lying comatose in bed for days. His arms felt like spaghetti, and at times his balance was off, however, with each day, he became stronger and started to feel a little more like his old self.

Henri accredited Dillon's survival to bulldogged determination and the fact he was in good shape to begin with. A weaker man would have succumbed to the thrashing by the alligator and the near fatal drowning.

Henri was right about the woods not being forgiving. Any of the bodies that had fallen in the swamp would have been ravaged by heat and scavengers within days, leaving little to find.

Holly kept rhythm with her horse's gait. She rode with an ease of only a seasoned rider; tall, elegant, regal, as if she shared the same purpose as the horse.

Dillon didn't have much experience with horses, only having ridden them as a child at dude ranches. On this trip he had come to trust Cowboy. He was a stocky horse, meant more for pulling a hayride wagon than a cross-country journey.

If it was possible for a rider to convey an emotional state to a horse, Dillon swore Cowboy had picked up on his anxiety. Cowboy's gait was steady and even, and when Dillon had approached the horse earlier, Cowboy had nudged him with his nose, offering comfort.

Chapter 6

A day after leaving Henri's fish camp, the ragged threesome stayed to the lesser travelled roads, away from civilization, skirting the bigger cities of Lafayette and Lake Charles, which had digressed into chaotic lawlessness.

They had to stop often to let Buster rest. The journey was beginning to take its toll.

Dillon's shoulders slumped and he held Cowboy's reins tight in his hands. His hair was damp under his cap, and he smelled of the woods and fire, of being in the country.

The sun cast long shadows through the trees, reaching out to the man and woman on horseback, and to the dog trotting alongside them.

Swampy humidity lingered in the air, and a tinge of pale yellow from the setting sun brushed the topmost leaves of the trees, through which the wind whistled.

"Let's make camp here," Dillon suggested.

He gathered a few rocks, put them in a circle, and arranged the kindling for a fire. The meager dinner didn't satiate the empty feeling in his stomach, and before he took the last bite of the rationed jerky, he gave it to Buster, hoping it would quell the dog's hunger pangs.

During the night, the constant gunfire they heard in the distance confirmed Dillon's suspicion of lawlessness in the larger cities.

Holly was snuggled into her bedroll, fully clothed, trying to ward off the night chill. Dillon was in the bedroll next to her, Buster lay curled near Dillon's feet, head tucked to his belly.

"I never noticed how bright the stars are," Holly remarked, unable to sleep.

"There is no ambient light from the cities. Have you ever noticed at night when you're traveling way out in the country, you can see the glow of the lights of the big cities on the horizon?"

"Can't say I've ever noticed," Holly said.

"It was always comforting to me when I drove at night," Dillon said, "knowing that even though I was miles and miles away, the city was within reach."

"What city?"

"Any city. It doesn't matter. They all have their unique culture and beat, yet with parallel narratives of people going about the business of living."

"What do you think is going on in the cities now?"

"Nothing good. It's the Wild West in the cities and whoever is the better armed will take control. Whoever has the most food will be attacked first. Unless the electrical grid magically reboots, it will be years before things get back to normal, if at all. If we're lucky, the United States won't be attacked, although I can't see China or Russia playing nice. It's like two roaming male lions trying to establish a new territory and as soon as weakness is detected, they go for the jugular. The result isn't pretty. The spoils of war go to the victor. The one good thing about the United States is the people are armed, and we will fight to keep our land. Back in the 60s and 70s, we underestimated the will of the North Vietnamese people, and like them, Russia and China don't know the will Americans possess.

"I'm guessing no one will attack us right away. They'll probably wait awhile until we are weakened from sickness or hunger, then they'll strike. There are too many unknowns right now."

"Like what?" Holly asked.

"Like if our military is still operational. Do our weapons still work? Satellites? Is communication still viable? Is the president still the commander in chief of our military? Those are the unknowns right now. Right now we'll have to worry about other things."

"Such as?"

"Such as what happens to the infrastructure of cities. Garbage won't be picked up and will soon overflow in the streets, attracting rats. Disease will be rampant. Plumbing will stop working after a bit. Grocery stores will be emptied by the end of the week, and medicine will be in short supply. People will be desperate because they'll need someone to guide them and instruct them what to do. There'll be people who want to take command and establish a new order. Fights will break out. Factions will develop."

"That sounds awful," Holly said.

"It will be. The lucky ones will hunker down and wait it out. That is, if they have enough supplies to last until new methods of transportation become available. Living by a river will literally be a lifesaver because an aluminum fishing boat with a gasoline powered motor will still be able to navigate shallow waterways, delivering supplies.

"I'm expecting the roads we need to take to your ranch will be blocked, so we'll have to either talk our way in, or find another way to get you home."

"You sound like you're going to drop me off. You can stay with me, Dillon. I'd like you to stay."

"I don't know. I feel like a vagabond right now. I don't even have a place to hang my hat."

"There're plenty of pegs on the wall inside the front door of my house where you can hang your hat."

The attempt at humor worked, because Dillon let out a whisper of a laugh.

"I'm serious, Dillon. What you did for me after the plane struck the courthouse, how you carried me all the way to your house, well, it meant a lot to me. You saved my life."

Dillon shrugged. "I would have done it for anybody."

"Maybe," Holly said. "But you didn't do it for just anybody. You did it for me. And the night we spent together, that meant more to me than you know."

"And to me," Dillon said.

The fire crackled, sending a spark of embers in the air, a flying squirrel glided on silent wings from treetop to treetop, and somewhere nearby a nighthawk squawked.

Holly was the first to speak. "Dillon, listen to me. I want you to know you mean a lot to me. We're a team now, not courtroom adversaries trying to outwit each other or get the judge's favor. Being together like this, day in and day out, I've learned a lot about you, and I like what I've found."

Dillon gazed at the dark sky and the immenseness of the universe. "I'm damaged, Holly, more than you know. Right when I thought I was getting over the death of my wife, I lost my daughter, my only child. It's more than I can handle. I've considered going back to Houston, but the more I think about it, the more I don't want to. My old life, the one with Amy and Cassie, was there. We made so many good memories. Everywhere I go, I would be thinking about them. I don't think I could bear being there by myself. And your home, is, well, just that. It's your home, not mine."

Holly thought about what 'home' meant to her. A place to call your own to escape the pressures of the day. A place to gather with family members sharing food and drink. Holly had lived, if it could be called that, biding time for what, she wasn't sure of. Maybe she had been waiting for someone like Dillon to share her home with.

She had observed Dillon in the courtroom when she didn't think he would notice, and she had learned a lot. She noticed the way he treated people, walking into a room, greeting them as if they were long lost friends. His energy was contagious, and after his wife died all Holly wanted to do was to tell him how sorry she was. She saw the grief etched into the deep lines on his face, and when he returned to work the spring in his step seemed a little less high.

Over time the raw grief had subsided.

Holly yearned for the moment she could muster up the courage to ask him out for coffee, something simple that didn't take much time. If conversation became difficult or if they had nothing in common it would be simple to check the time, making an excuse to see a client.

But that never happened. They went from zero to sixty in one night.

"We can make it *our* home, Dillon," Holly said sincerely. "Please tell me you'll stay, because I've been thinking about what you said."

"What was that?"

"About leaning on each other. That it's okay to help each other, to need each other." Taking her hand out of the sleeping bag, she held it open to him, willing him to take it. "We are making our own memories now."

The night was quiet. A breeze rustled the leaves, the sky was inky, trees black against the night.

Rising, Holly went to sit next to Dillon. Wisps of hair blew across her face and she tucked them behind her ear.

Dillon sat up, reached over to Holly, and cupped her face in his hands.

She put her hand to his and leaned her face into him.

The simple connection with another human being brought Dillon back to the moment and the journey regarding how he had come to know the real Holly Hudson. This woman, who he had only known in the courtroom with her manicured nails and perfectly coiffed hair, had risked her life to save him. She had biked over a hundred miles while fighting a deadly infection without complaining. She had shown the same tenacity and bullheadedness when she waded into the water to save him without regard for her own life. Somehow she'd made a litter out of sticks and rope, tied him in and secured it to his horse, and had retraced their steps back to the fish camp. The determination and work required spoke loud and clear, more than a thousand words ever could.

"I love you," Dillon said.

"I love you too," Holly said.

Dillon leaned into Holly and put his hand around the nape of her neck, pulling her closer. Her lips parted naturally, and he leaned in and kissed her softly at first, no more than a feather brushing the wind. Then he kissed her fully on the lips, the way a man should kiss a woman, a strong kiss, filled with passion and need. She returned an equally passionate kiss, and they stayed like that, their lips touching as the dim light from the campfire flickered, sending shadows dancing into the night.

He stood and pulled Holly up with him.

There were no words, only the fire crackling in the quiet night.

She removed her socks and set them aside, undid her belt and set it on the ground.

Dillon removed his shirt and draped it over a scrubby bush. Taking a step closer to Holly, he helped her with the buttons on her shirt, and together they removed their remaining clothes.

The cool air tingled their skin, and Dillon kissed the tip of her nose, her cheeks and neck, moving his hands along her body, taking his time.

Goosebumps appeared on Holly and she shivered.

"Let's get in the sleeping bag," Dillon said, "and warm each other up."

* * *

"Let's try to get some sleep so we can get an early start," Dillon said an hour later. "If we leave by daybreak, we should be back at your ranch by noon."

Dillon and Holly fell asleep in their respective sleeping bags. The night crept forward, stars shifted in the heavens, the campfire dwindled to coals.

Sometime during the night, Dillon woke and lay on his back, thinking of his family and of Cassie's short life. A life lived, even a short one, was better than none at all, and he had been honored to have been Cassie's father. He replayed the important events in her life, first day of school, soccer games, school plays. Her first date, senior prom, acceptance letters to college. All only memories now.

His eyelids were getting heavy and his thoughts drifted to her friends and how they were coping without texting, the internet, or cable TV. A slight smile crept across his face as he thought about how the younger generation would have to resort to good old face to face communication.

An owl hooted somewhere nearby. Dillon was warm in his bedroll, Holly was sleeping peacefully, Buster by his side, the horses staked close by…

Dillon's eyes popped wide open and he sat up bolt straight. He looked over at Holly. "You asleep?"

"Hmm," she said, stifling a yawn. "What's going on?"

"My daughter was flying with her best friend, Vicky."

"I know," Holly said. "I'm sorry what happened to her. Maybe there is some way we can get in touch with her parents to tell them."

"No, that's not what I'm talking about. You don't understand," Dillon said. There was definite urgency in his voice.

"What?" Holly propped herself up on her elbows. "What are you talking about?"

"From the time they were little, people mistook Vicky and Cassie for sisters because they looked so much alike. They were the same height, weight, straight brown hair, same complexion."

"Okay, so?" Holly rubbed her forehead.

"It's possible the survivor who said he saw Cassie thrown out of the plane could have mistaken her for Vicky. They were traveling together so would have sat next to each other."

Holly said nothing, only stared at Dillon.

"It could have been Vicky who died, not Cassie."

Chapter 7

"I think the United States has been attacked," Ryan said.

Well, *that* got James's and Garrett's attention. James swallowed a gulp of coffee, while Garrett stared at Ryan in disbelief, their minds whirling, trying to figure out what country might be the aggressor.

"I haven't seen any fighter jets," Garrett said.

"Not yet," Ryan replied. "That'll be later. Whoever was responsible has set the wheels in motion to dismantle the infrastructure of the United States."

"Using what?" Garrett asked. "Germ warfare?"

"I don't think so. That would only take out a concentrated area, like New York. And I don't think it would specifically be an all-out ground and air war with paratroopers and—"

"Like in *Red Dawn*," James interrupted. "I saw that movie."

"Me too," Garrett said. "Swayze kicked butt in that movie."

They all agreed and laughed.

Ryan said, "We wouldn't see jets screaming overhead or foreign soldiers invading our land using parachutes. It would be something more devious and deadly. Something that would cripple the United States." He got up from the table and poured another cup of coffee, put a spoonful of sugar in it and stirred it around, clinking the sides. He sat back down at the table. "Let's go over what we do know. The plane we were on lost power for no explainable reason. Our cell phones are dead, the landline only works intermittently. There's no electricity, and Garrett's truck won't start. That only means one thing."

The room became quiet and the expressions on their faces were of worry and incredulity.

"The electrical grid has been disabled by an electromagnetic pulse bomb," Ryan surmised. "EMP for short."

Garrett leaned back in his chair while James sat in stunned silence. Cassie's and Adelaide's muted conversation and laughter from outside echoed into the house while the innocent game of fetch Skeeter was playing with Gumbo seemed surreal against the realization of the upcoming societal breakdown.

A fly buzzed into the house and landed on the kitchen table. Ryan shooed it away.

"I've read about that," Garrett said. "I may have lived in the swamp all my life, but I've read about that." He got up from the table and scanned the bookshelves, selecting a book. "It's in this one." He thumped the cover. "It would explain why the phones are out too. Back in the mid-1800s a huge solar flare, now named the Carrington Event, took out telegraph lines. The northern lights were seen as far south as Cuba."

"You're making that up," James protested.

"I'm not," Garrett said, handing him the book. "An EMP would work on the same premise and it would fry anything with a computer board, like what's in modern cars, which explains why I haven't seen or heard any cars on the road, except for old man Heafford who drives a 1930s truck." He ran his hands over his beard. "Jesus Christ Almighty. In our high tech world, we are for a shit storm."

"I know," Ryan said.

"That explains a lot. Why my truck won't start. Why the electricity is out. Me, and my family," Garrett said, "we'll be okay. We can live off the land. I can hunt and fish. I can trade with other folks who can't. I've got books to school my grandson. The winter's not too bad where we are. Summers are a beast, though, with the heat and mosquitoes. We can make it. We're tough, made from good stock." Garrett gazed out the window at his daughter-in-law, grandson, and Cassie doing everyday normal things. "What about you, James? You've been awful quiet. What do you think?"

"I've never heard about an EMP or the Carrington Event, but if what this book says is true, we're in for a hard time if the electrical grid is down." He set the book on the table. "Every modern convenience runs off of electricity. I've lived in the city all my life, never hunted, only fished a couple of times. I'll be useless." He hung his head.

"What do you do for a livin'?" Garrett asked.

"Lawnmower salesman. I was traveling to Atlanta for a lawnmower convention." He shook his head. "I wasn't even supposed to go, but at the last minute my boss said I'd been working too hard, and to use the convention as R&R. Yeah. Some vacation."

"Stop feeling sorry for yourself. You're alive, which is a whole lot better than the rest of the people on that plane who are gator bait by now," Garrett said gruffly.

"I suppose so," James said.

"Do you know how to repair lawnmowers?" Garrett asked.

"Yes," James said. "I've tinkered with all sorts of things since I was a kid. When I was five I took apart the grandfather clock in our living room because I wanted to know how it worked." He chuckled. "My mom wasn't too happy about it. I progressed to engines when I was a teenager, but if engines don't work, I won't be of much use."

Garrett's gaze swiveled from James to Ryan, who had been sitting quietly. "I have an idea. Come with me," Garrett said.

Walking out of the house, Garrett called to his daughter-in-law that they would be back in a few minutes.

"Breakfast will be ready soon," Adelaide said. "So don't be long."

Garrett led them around the back of the house, past the chicken coop to a large wooden shack which also doubled as a barn. It was where Garrett kept the farming relics passed down from his grandfather to his father, and then to him.

With great effort, he slid open the double doors. Sunlight illuminated the cavernous interior showing a loft with hay bales, a plethora of rusty farm equipment, including a plow that could be old enough to have been used before the Great Depression. A pile of mason jars littered one corner along with a pair of tattered overalls in which a rat had made a nest. Garrett invited them to walk further in.

He pushed aside a pickaxe, a metal rake, and a grubbing hoe. He wiggled around more relics including an ox yoke, the leather old and cracked.

"Are you looking for something?" Ryan asked.

"As a matter of fact, yes. Come see," Garrett said.

"What?" Ryan asked. "That?" He pointed to an ancient automobile sitting on blocks.

"Here is where James comes in handy," Garrett said.

James immediately perked up and gave the old truck a onceover. "It's about a 1940 something Ford truck." He ran a finger over the grille. "This grille was a signature of the Ford. It's a classic style with rimmed tire wells and a small bed." James glanced at Garrett. "If what you said about modern cars that have a computer board is true—"

"You're not useless after all," Garrett said. A big smile broke across his face and he tossed a knowing look at Ryan.

"Wait a moment," James said, realizing the implication. "You want me to fix *that*?"

"Smart man."

Chapter 8

James instructed Ryan and Garrett to clear away the junk from around the truck.

"First thing we need to do is to get it off the blocks. I need to check the structural integrity of the truck and I need to be able to move freely. I don't want anything falling on me. I'll also need you to clear a path out of the barn so we can move it. I'll work outside because I can't see anything in here. It's too dark."

While Ryan and Garrett worked to clear away the junk, James made a visual check of the truck. Surprisingly, it hadn't rusted that much and the rust he did see didn't affect the safety of the truck. The tires were flat, though.

"You have a tire pump?" he asked.

"I do," Garrett replied.

Opening the door, James inspected the interior. The seats were still in fairly good condition, the instrument panels were visible under a coating of dust. Garrett handed James the tire pump. While James pumped up each tire, the other two cleared away more junk. Thankfully, the tires held the air pressure.

"We're good to go!" James called.

With the path cleared, James sat in the driver's side and checked for the keys. There were none, so he felt around under the seat. Bingo. He put the truck in neutral then glanced in the review mirror. Ryan and Garrett were standing at the end of the bed, waiting for instruction. James gave a thumbs-up. "Start pushing!"

Placing their hands on each end of the truck bed, Garrett counted. "One, two," he took a big breath before saying "threeee!" With a steady heave, the truck lurched forward an inch, then a foot, squeaking and moaning, bouncing along the uneven dirt floor of the barn. The wheels protested the movement as if it was awakening from a long, deep slumber.

Slowly, Ryan and Garrett pushed the truck out of the barn and onto the grassy land.

The early morning sun was blinding, and Ryan shaded his eyes, squinting. It took his eyes several seconds to adjust to the bright sun. "If this thing had been a mole, it would be blind about now," he laughed.

James exited the truck and shut the door. "Good work," he said, high-fiving each man. "Can we eat breakfast? I'm going to need some fuel before I can work on this. And I'm going to need a can of gas, motor oil, and a battery."

"I'll get those for you," Garrett said.

"Also, for a truck this old, I'll need a six volt battery." Looking around, James spied a tractor sitting on the other side of the orchard. "The battery from that tractor will do."

* * *

After breakfast, the men excused themselves to resume working on the truck. Skeeter and Gumbo trotted along after them, leaving Cassie and Adelaide in the kitchen. Cassie helped clear the dishes while Adelaide scraped the leftover scraps into Gumbo's food bowl. Filling a large bowl with water, Adelaide washed the plates and tableware, handing the clean dishes to Cassie to dry.

"It's not any of my business, and you don't have to answer me if you don't want to," Adelaide said, "but are you and Ryan a couple?"

The question took Cassie by surprise. "No. When you're trying to survive, there isn't much time to think about a Saturday night date."

"Maybe not, but I noticed the way he was looking at you. It's the way a guy looks at a girl he's interested in."

For a while neither said anything. Cassie considered the question. Perhaps in any other circumstance, like having a class together or meeting him via mutual friends, she and Ryan may have been a couple. He had seen her at her worst—dirty, sweaty, hungry, smelly clothes—so if he had been thinking about her in any other way, it would astonish her.

Apocalypse or not, Cassie needed to clean herself up.

"Where can I take a bath?" she asked.

"There's a spigot and a hose on the side of the pump house," Adelaide said. "Water's going to be cold though."

"I don't care. I'm so filthy, even if I had to jump in an ice lake to get clean, I'd do it."

Adelaide gave Cassie a towel, clean clothes to wear, a bar of soap, and a bottle of shampoo.

Walking down the back porch steps on her way to the pump house, Cassie glanced at the guys working on the vintage truck. They had decided over breakfast that if James got the truck working, Garrett would drive them into town so they could get decent camping supplies for the rest of their journey home.

The hood was propped open and James was leaning into the engine. Garrett stood to the side, holding a surplus of tools, while Ryan was the gopher running back and forth into the barn, fetching more tools.

Standing behind the pump house, out of view of everyone, Cassie stripped off her dirty clothes. She set them on the ground, sprinkled them with the hose, then gave them a vigorous scrubbing with the bar of soap. A nearby branch worked well as a clothesline, which was where she hung her clothes to dry. She peeked from around the corner of the pump house to make sure the guys were still busy at the truck.

So far so good. She went about the business of getting clean, scrubbing off a thick layer of Louisiana swamp mud and enough grime to last a lifetime.

At the truck James asked for a bucket of water so he could clean away a half century worth of gunk.

"There's a bucket inside the barn on the right. You can fill it up with water at the spigot behind the pump house," Garrett said.

"There still should be enough water pressure from the generator running this morning. We needed water for breakfast and washing dishes."

"I'll get it," Ryan replied.

He darted to the barn, grabbed the bucket, and headed to the pump house. When he rounded the corner he stopped dead in his tracks. There was Cassie in her glorious birthday suit, soap bubbles dripping down her back, her clean skin glistening in the sunlight. Her head was at an angle as she ran her fingers through her hair, untangling it.

Ryan knew he should do the gentlemanly thing and leave, but wild horses couldn't drag him away from taking in the curve of her hips and those long legs that he had imagined being wrapped around him.

Ryan's heart pumped about as fast as when the plane took a nosedive. He stood there uncertain what to do. Should he leave and come back, talking loud so Cassie would have warning he was coming? It wasn't like he'd never seen any naked women before, but the sight of the woman who had been on his mind for the past three days was something he couldn't turn away from. He sure did like what he saw and—

Without warning, Cassie turned around and locked eyes with him. Her eyes went wide and she made a feeble attempt to cover herself with her hands. "Oh my God!" she shrieked. "Turn around! Now!"

Ryan looked away and covered his eyes with his hand. He turned his back to her. "Sorry," he mumbled.

"How long have you been standing there watching me!" She grabbed the towel and wrapped it around herself.

"I didn't see anything. I…I…uh…" Ryan stammered with his back to Cassie, unable to get the image of her naked body out of his mind.

"You saw everything!" Cassie screeched. "You can turn around. I'm covered up now."

Ryan turned around. "I'm sorry. Garrett asked me to get a bucket of water. I swear," he said putting up a hand, "I didn't know you were here bathing, uh, naked." He glanced down and scratched the back of his neck, which was itching for some reason.

"Seriously? How else does somebody take a bath?" Cassie

clasped the towel edges together with one hand, while the other hand was planted on her hip.

Ryan burst out laughing.

"What's so funny?" Cassie demanded.

"Nothing. Nothing at all."

"What!"

"You should have seen the expression on your face."

Cassie remained silent, glaring at him.

"And," Ryan said, dropping his voice, "if you must know, you look really good naked."

Cassie didn't know whether to laugh or smack him for being such a dolt. For a long moment they stood there staring at each other until Cassie made the first move. Walking toward him, clasping the towel around her, she brushed his arm with hers. She gave him an approving onceover, letting her eyes settle on his.

Ryan held her resolute gaze.

With one mischievous eyebrow raised, Cassie said, "I bet you look really good naked too."

Chapter 9

"Dillon," Holly said, "don't do this to yourself. Cassie's gone, and going back into the swamp won't do any good. You're still not one hundred percent. I saw you nod off several times while riding yesterday, and I hate to say this, but her...body would have been reclaimed by now. Ashes to ashes, dust to dust. Earth to Earth. You know what I'm talking about, right?"

"I'm not ready to listen to a funeral eulogy. I won't believe she's gone until I find her body," Dillon said. It aggravated him that Holly brought this up. He had held on to fleeting hope and he'd be damned if anyone told him otherwise.

"You had her for twenty-four years, now she belongs to someone else. If it's any consolation, she's with her mother and our Heavenly Father." Holly tried to be as comforting as she could.

Dillon put his hand up to stop her. "I don't want to hear it."

Holly opened her mouth to say something else then decided against it. She couldn't imagine what it must be like to lose a child. Yet in a way she did, because she had lost a child in her own way. Her child was alive at least, which she couldn't say to Dillon.

She stretched out in the sleeping bag. The night was dark and the stars were bright in the sky, twinkling in the heavens. Gazing upon them, the immenseness of the galaxy struck her, and she suddenly felt insignificant. Though she couldn't tell if his eyes were open, Dillon's breathing was steady and even, and he must be tired to the bone after all he had been through. His bruised body would eventually heal in time, but she had no idea how long it would take for his heart to heal, if it ever would.

His emotional wound was too raw and new, and it would be foolish to try to force any sort of closure on him.

Listening to him breathing comforted Holly, and she felt safe with him, as if nothing could harm her. At her apartment, even with people sleeping on the other side of a shared wall, she rarely got a good night's sleep. Little noises like a dish clinking in the sink or a book shifting on the bookshelves caused her to wake and listen for other noises.

She'd expected she would feel safer living in the 'burbs in a house with an alarm system, but she never had.

In the wide open country without walls or a roof, she felt at peace, a peace she had longed for, and Dillon was now part of that.

Holly had tried to persuade Dillon to rest and get stronger for a few more days, to let his body completely heal before undertaking the grueling two day ride back to her ranch. Unfortunately, her words of wisdom fell on deaf ears. He was a strong and stubborn man, and Holly admired him for that, although there were moments it drove her bat-shit crazy.

In the long night a breeze with a hint of salty swamp came through, brushing the land and the trees. An owl hooted long and lonely, and Holly drifted off to sleep.

* * *

A few minutes before daybreak, Dillon woke, startled by a nearby noise. After listening intently, he surmised it had only been a nocturnal animal, possibly an armadillo or a possum. Holly was still sleeping. A brief reluctance came to him and he regretted his surliness the previous evening.

He shrugged out of the sleeping bag. Stretching, he took in the land, listening to the sounds of the world awakening. A dove cooed, songbirds chirped a morning melody, and the low sun reached across the land, casting long fingers of warmth.

Buster lay curled in a tight ball on top of the sleeping bag, his fur dewy and cold from the night. He lazily opened one eye and looked at his owner. The dog had become lean from the long days of trotting beside the horses. The comfortable times of loafing on a cushiony sofa had become a distant memory for the dog, and after spending days together with his pack, studying their body language and voice intonation, he understood them more.

Buster lifted his head and sniffed the air. His owner was experiencing some sort of emotional stress, and his canine instinct told him to stay near.

Dillon stretched his sore muscles and body. He had been restless during the night, turning and tossing while vivid dreams interrupted any sleep. He briefly remembered Amy in one of his dreams, but for the life of him he couldn't recall what had happened. At the time the dream had seemed profound, as if she was trying to tell him something important, yet the dream was too foggy.

He shook off the dream and the morning chill.

During the night Dillon had come to realize the futility in continuing the search for Cassie. If she was alive she would have walked out of the swamp. As her father, he had prepared her for being lost. He had taught her how to make a shelter using low-hanging branches that could be torn from a tree. He had taught her how to make a fire using rudimentary tools of a knife or another sharp instrument, kindling, and a good rock. He had shown her what berries and roots in the wild were edible, not exactly the kind of calories needed for long term survival, but in a pinch, they'd do.

If what the survivor Henri took in had said was true, she might have indeed been a casualty of the plane crash. The chances of her walking out of the swamp alone, and without proper gear, weren't good either. He had always told Cassie she was made from good stock because with a surname of "Stockdale," she couldn't be anything else.

Without any landmarks to guide her, it would be too easy for Cassie to become disoriented in the flat land of Louisiana, especially if clouds obscured the sun.

Dillon still couldn't bring himself to say she was dead. Casualty sounded softer, less final.

He reached down and picked up a handful of sandy dirt. Walking away from the campsite he followed an animal trail, wending a path through the high grass and around trees for thirty yards or so to a clearing.

Buster padded silently behind, ignoring the smells of the woodland that beckoned to him.

Dillon plucked a stand of late-blooming yellow flowers. The sun streamed through the trees, and a gentle breeze blew. Kneeling on one knee he hung his head and whispered, “Calista Ann Stockdale,” letting the silty dirt sift through his fingers, falling onto the dewy grass.

Ashes to ashes. Dust to dust…

Dillon tried in vain to remember the rest of the prayer, and the weight of his grief crashed down upon him. This was the first time he had allowed himself to experience any pain, always being stoic, never letting anyone witness his private agony after his wife died. He put his hand to his forehead and wept openly at the loss of his family.

Sensing the overwhelming grief Dillon was experiencing, Buster came up to him and nudged him with a wet nose. He put his chin on Dillon’s knee. Dillon stroked him long and thoughtfully on the back, from the nape of his neck to his tail, smoothing down the rough fur. The simple connection soothed Dillon, and Buster felt Dillon release a big breath.

“It’s only you and me, boy. Everyone else is gone. I don’t even know how to go on. How to live. I feel old and worn out, like there’s no purpose.”

Buster kept his chin on Dillon’s knee, listening to the sad sounds his owner made. Buster had followed him into the clearing because he sensed there was purpose to the short jaunt, and he sensed his owner shouldn’t be alone.

After the alligator attack, Dillon hadn’t been the same.

His body was slowly healing, and Buster recognized the casual gait that replaced the stiff posture.

Although Buster couldn’t discern the meaning of the lines etched into Dillon’s face, he did sense an inner struggle his owner faced. It had happened after an emotional conversation of loud voices and angry stares at the old man’s fish camp.

Buster smelled Dillon’s muscles rejuvenating and becoming stronger. The limp had disappeared, but the facial lines told an entirely different story, one of sadness and loss.

Though Buster had never met the woman who lived with Dillon, her essence had been left everywhere in the house, and at one time she must have been his mate. A lock of hair, clothes hanging in the closet, shoes neatly stacked in the closet. Buster checked the smell of any female who came to the house, searching for the one who had left so much. He had never been able to identify any female as *the one*, and after a while, her scent diminished to the point it had disappeared.

Then this new woman had come home with his owner.

As a dog, his senses alerted him to the unusual pheromones the female released while she talked to Dillon. While Buster kept his head on Dillon's knee, he was aware that Dillon intermittently released his own male scent. At times it was stronger than others, and Buster had a flash of memory when his owner brought the injured woman home. There had been numerous conflicting signals each gave to the other.

In the end, the humans had remained together, and Buster considered them his pack.

He preferred his new pack, even the new woman, and his canine instinct would protect them and alert them to danger by using his superior scents of sight, sound, and smell.

Dillon cleared his throat and stood up. He blinked several times then wiped his face with the back of his hand. "Come on, boy, let's go."

The sun brightened the sky where low clouds floated on the horizon. The horses stood nearby, relaxed, nibbling on grass and the occasional dandelion, clover, and other edible weeds.

Dillon went to the horses and fed them several handfuls of oats.

By now, Holly was up and had prepared breakfast consisting of sliced peaches and deer jerky slapped between two pieces of homemade bread. Dillon broke off a piece of bread and gave it to Buster, who gobbled it like it was his last meal. Afterwards, Dillon gave Buster the last of the dog food. When Holly looked away, Dillon slipped Buster a piece of jerky.

Holly ate in silence on the opposite side of the campfire.

"Let's get going," Dillon said after breakfast was eaten.

Holly rounded up the horses and put the saddle and bridle on each of them while Dillon packed their bedrolls and kicked dirt over the fire.

Dillon eased into Cowboy's saddle and when the horse felt his weight, he stood at attention, waiting patiently for the magic phrase.

"Ride 'em Cowboy," Dillon said without much conviction, followed by a quick kick in the flanks.

For a while they travelled in silence, Holly by Dillon's side, the horses stepping in rhythm, man and woman keeping private thoughts. They were equal partners now, each having their own tasks to do, and most of all they had each other's backs. The way a man and woman should be; one complements the other's shortcomings.

The ride gave Holly more time to think. It was easier to figure out Dillon when he talked, and this silent treatment was befuddling to her. She knew he was a man of meaningful words, eloquent in his speaking, having personally witnessed his persuasive and oratory abilities in the courtroom.

Either he needed an audience or he was suffering immensely. She suspected the latter.

They rode in silence along the lonely blacktop road. Holly had suggested this route because it was rarely used during normal times. After several hours, they rounded a bend, nearing the bridge over the languid and murky Sabine River, which was the eastern boundary line between Louisiana and Texas. On the other side was Sabine County where Holly's ranch was located.

Dillon pulled up Cowboy's reins, stopping the horse, motioning for Holly to do the same. He put an index finger to his mouth for her to be quiet. He pointed to the direction of the bridge where several armed men were patrolling, and by their appearance, they weren't going to let anyone in.

"This is bad," Dillon whispered.

"Maybe we should go downstream and try to find a place to cross," Holly suggested.

"That only works in the movies. This river is deceptively peaceful. In reality it's a death trap. It's deep and has a strong flow. See those ripples?" He pointed to the other side. "That's the equivalent of a riptide. You get caught in that and you'll drown."

"Then let's go up there and talk to them."

"Not both of us. You stay back here, out of sight, and if anything happens to me you ride out of here as fast as you can."

"Dillon, I—"

"No." Dillon gave her a pointed look that was all business. "Stay out of sight. I mean it."

"Okay," Holly said reluctantly.

Dillon rode out into the open, away from the trees, away from cover. One of the men hollered to the other two, and all three coalesced in front of the bridge.

"Whoa, that's far enough," one of the men said.

Dillon brought Cowboy to a halt. He glanced at the men, gauging their character by the way they carried themselves. If they had been horses, the phrase, "rode hard and put up wet" would have done justice to their appearance. Scraggly beards, sweat-stained shirts, pants hadn't seen the inside of a washing machine in a long while.

The one who spoke was obviously the leader. He carried a pump action 12 gauge shotgun, and stood in front of the other two, who nervously glanced at the guy as if they needed to be told what to do.

"I don't want any trouble," Dillon said. "I only want to cross. May I?"

"That depends," the man said. His two cohorts backed him up by nodding and showing their scratched Winchester 30-30s that had probably been carelessly thrown into the bed of a truck countless times.

Dillon could discern what a man was like by the way he treated his weapons. Firearms took time to clean. A dirty gun that jammed or misfired was useless. These bozos probably didn't even know what a chamber brush was. They didn't impress him at all, and were obviously lazy.

"On what?" Dillon asked.

"Well, you see…" the man hocked a wad of tobacco into the grass, "we're not lettin' strangers or riffraff into our county. Only residents are gettin' to cross. So unless you can prove you live here, go back to wherever you came from."

Dillon shifted in the saddle, not exactly sure what to say.

"And you can tell your lady friend to come out from behind the trees. My spotter—"

"Spotter?"

"Sittin' in a tree yonder," the man said, motioning with his head.

Dillon swiveled his gaze, checking the trees. A towering pine caught his attention. Squinting, his eyes followed the tree until he found the man. He was sitting on a makeshift ledge made out of two by fours nailed into a high branch. Dillon cursed silently at having been so careless to have missed the spotter. He'd have to be careful to have all his wits about him from now on.

"You've been in the crosshairs of a LaRue OBR sniper rifle for some time."

"An AR-15 on steroids," Dillon remarked.

"You know your weapons. My spotter let us know two riders were coming this way." The man cupped his hand to his mouth and shouted in the direction of his spotter, "Chandler, come on down!" Turning back to Dillon, he said, "So if you got nothin' to hide, then why did your lady friend stay behind?"

"Maybe you're the riffraff, not us," Dillon said. He made a motion to position his AK for firing.

"Hey! Keep your hands where we can see them."

Dillon mulled over his chances of getting off a shot and whether or not Holly would be next. He was outnumbered and outgunned. Reluctantly, he moved his hands away from his AK.

"Pardon my manners. I totally forgot to introduce us. That's Cyrus and Don, and I'm Frank. There now," Frank said, hitching up his britches. "We aren't riffraff, are we boys? And looky here, there's the rest of my quad. This here is Chandler."

Dillon quickly sized up the man walking toward them. He wasn't as backwoods as the rest of his cohorts, and had a certain edge to him that Dillon recognized. He was tall and athletic, unlike the rest of the quad he was associated with who were nearly as wide as they were tall.

Dillon's eyes immediately went to the rifle. An OBR—the Texas answer to the search for the perfect semi-automatic sniper rifle. Topped with a Nightforce scope and loaded with 20 rounds of 308 Winchester 175 grain Hollow Point Boat Tail match ammo, anyone within 800 meters was in serious danger. Made in Leander, Texas, the OBR had the classical AR-10 profile with the kind of custom tweaks that perfectly mated precision with reliability.

"We have jobs," Cyrus said. "Riffraff don't."

Dillon thought about that a second. Maybe it *wasn't* a bad idea to close up the county until things settled down. Since they hadn't asked for any tolls, maybe these guys were on the up and up. He called, "Holly, you can come on out."

Holly coaxed her horse onto the blacktop, calling for Buster to follow. Coming alongside Cowboy, she stopped.

"They need proof that we live in the county," Dillon said, "before they let us cross."

"Like what?" Holly asked. "A driver's license?"

"That'll do," Frank said.

"Didn't bring it with me," Holly said. "Cars aren't exactly working. Last I checked a horse license isn't necessary."

"A horse license!" Frank bellowed. He slapped a knee and doubled over, letting out a belly laugh. "Now that's an idea. I think I'll start my own business of collecting fees for horse licenses."

"I own a ranch in the western part of the county," Holly said tersely.

"So?" Frank said. "Any yahoo can claim that. Got proof?"

"No. Forgot the deed too."

Frank smirked. "You sure do have a smart mouth on you for such a pretty lady. I like my women, how should I say ...subservient."

"Big word for a small man," Holly shot back.

Frank smiled, but without humor. "Besides, we're not letting anyone in who is contagious..." He eyed Dillon suspiciously. "You look peaked, like you got the fever or somethin'."

"I'm not sick," Dillon said. "I got attacked by an alligator and almost died. I'm still recovering."

"You expect me to believe that?" Frank asked. "There aren't any gators this far inland."

"He *did* get attacked," Holly confirmed. "It happened in the Atchafalaya Basin. He has the bruises to prove it, and," she said, digging around in her knapsack, "here are the alligator teeth in case you don't believe me." She held up a string of large teeth.

Dillon was surprised Holly kept them.

"A souvenir, courtesy of our trip," Holly said.

"Lemme see those," Frank said. He sidled up to Holly's horse and inspected the teeth.

Buster growled low in his throat, showing his teeth when Frank approached Holly.

"You can tell your old cur to back off," Frank said.

"Buster!" Dillon made direct eye contact with his dog. "No!"

The dog eyed the man suspiciously. A good judge of character,

Buster had picked up the smells of testosterone-laced sweat mixed with cheap alcohol. It was different than the kind of drink Dillon consumed at home, the kind that chilled him out after a hard day. The type of liquor the man had consumed was foul-smelling and bitter, and the man acted like he was a male alpha, stronger and braver than Buster's pack leader.

Buster had been on the road long enough to gauge the quality of humans he came in contact with. This man had an evil way about him, by the sounds he made and his taunting laugh, and Buster especially noticed the way the man had eyed Holly, like she was a piece of meat he wanted to eat. Holly was Dillon's mate, and though Buster had no concept of a marriage, Buster knew the two were a pack, and Buster was now part of that pack.

The dog kept back as he was instructed but if prodded, he'd jump on that man like a mongoose on a cobra and tear his throat out.

Frank inspected the teeth. "I believe you're telling me the truth. Seen those kind of teeth for sale at the tackle shop in town. What exactly were you doing in the Atchafalaya Basin?"

"Trying to find my daughter," Dillon said.

"In the swamp? That doesn't make any sense." Frank cast a dubious look at his group.

"She was on a plane when the EMP struck," Dillon said. It would have lost power and crash landed."

Frank made eye contact with Chandler.

Chandler asked, "What do you know about the EMP?"

Dillon briefly explained that the electrical grid went down and that anything powered by a computer would be toast.

"I already know all that," Chandler said. "Do you know who was responsible?"

"No."

"I'm guessing it was Iran or Iraq."

"Possibly," Dillon said. "I'm thinking the Russians might be behind this, but it hasn't been my top priority to try to figure out who is behind the attack. I've been concentrating on finding my daughter."

"Did you?"

Dillon glanced at the ground. He couldn't bring himself to say she was dead, especially to strangers who were butting into his private life. "We didn't find her, and from what we learned, she probably didn't survive the airplane crash."

"I'm sorry to hear that," Chandler said.

Dillon shifted in the saddle. "Nice rifle you got there. You military?"

Chandler nodded. "Saw action in Kandahar. When my tour was up last year, I came home to find my girlfriend shacked up with my best friend. I beat the shit out of him, then when she tried to make up with me I told her she could go to Hell." Chandler paused, waiting for Dillon's reaction.

Dillon shrugged. "Don't blame you. I probably would have done the same thing. Sorry to hear about your girlfriend and your best friend."

"Don't be. I got out of jail last week and had made plans to go back to Central Texas where my family lives when the EMP hit. I'm stuck here for a while. Are you military?"

"Ex-military. Medic in the Gulf War."

Chandler ran a hand through his hair. "Then I consider you family. I'm Chris Chandler." He extended a hand. "Call me Chandler, everybody else does."

"Dillon Stockdale," he said, shaking hands. He jerked his head to Holly. "Holly Hudson."

Holly nodded a greeting.

Half listening to the conversation, when Frank heard Dillon introduce himself and Holly, he just about shit in his pants. "What did you say your names were?"

Holly and Dillon exchanged wary glances. Either this was going to go really good, or really bad.

Chapter 10

Dillon repeated their names.

"That's what I thought you said," Frank replied. "You're those fancy lawyers involved in the Cole Cassel case."

Dillon swiveled his eyes from Frank to the rest of the goons who had brought up their rifles. From the tone of Frank's voice and the rifles pointing at him, this was going to go badly. "Cassel was on trial for murder."

"I know that," Frank said. "So he did the world a favor and got rid of a lowlife, who cares?"

"The justice system does," Dillon said.

"And you were a champion for that, right? The one prosecuting him. Your lady friend over there was the one defending him, and from what I've heard, she wasn't doing that good of a job."

Holly threw a sneer in Frank's direction.

"You sound like you have inside information," Dillon said.

Holly sat stoically on her horse as the conversation went downhill. She had saved Dillon's hide once before under much different circumstances, but wasn't sure about taking on three guys who had the edge, not to mention Chandler, who had been their sniper lookout. She briefly considered going for her 45, ultimately deciding against it. Her eyes dropped to Dillon's AK, knowing if he made any fast moves for the rifle, he'd be shot dead. She had the 45 in a holster on her hip. It would take too long to reach for it and sight in on one of the goons, so she sat still and let Dillon do the talking.

"Actually, I do have inside information." Frank spat another mouthful of tobacco into the grass. "The boss said there's a large reward in it for whoever brings you in. Dead or alive."

Dillon's eyes darted to the two goons flanking Frank. A shotgun blast at this range could kill both him and Cowboy, and while Dillon would sacrifice a horse for his life, he wasn't willing to gamble at the moment. Holly had certainly been unprepared for the ambush, and Dillon cursed his stupidity at letting his emotions getting the best of him. He'd have to use his wits to get out of this dilemma, especially the *wanted dead or alive* part.

"Who's the boss?" Dillon asked. He needed to stall for time and formulate a plan. He suspected he already knew who the boss was, but it would be better if he kept that bit of knowledge to himself. If he could keep Frank engaged long enough, it might give him an advantage. Talking and shooting required the use of both brain hemispheres, and multi-tasking didn't appear to be one of Frank's better qualities. Dillon doubted he could talk and shoot at the same time.

"That's for me to know and for you to find out," Frank said haughtily. He idly scratched his beard and gazed wantonly at Holly sitting high and mighty on her horse. He licked his lips, his gaze dropping down to Holly's thighs and to the *V* of her womanliness warming the hard saddle.

Holly shifted uncomfortably in the saddle then sat taller, challenging his leering stare.

A corner of Frank's mouth lifted in a knowing smirk and something stirred in him. He winked, and Holly gave him a defiant glare, then turned away in disgust.

"Come on," Dillon said, "you've already got us, might as well tell me who you are working for."

Frank mulled that over in his caveman brain. "Yeah, I guess it won't do no harm. You'll know soon enough. The boss is Cole Cassel, and—"

The rifle shot caught everyone off guard, and it took a long second for the group to comprehend what had happened.

The force of the bullet knocked Frank off his horse. His shotgun went flying and he fell facedown onto the dirt, where a crimson stain soaked the dirt from his motionless chest. The bullet had entered his chest, tearing through it and slicing his spine. A ragged, gaping hole was left where the bullet exited. Frank's right hand twitched and his upper body stiffened before going slack and falling still.

Two more rifle cracks caught the second and third guy of Frank's quad off guard, sending them to an early grave.

Dillon leapt off his horse and scrambled through high grass then behind a tree. "Take cover!" he screamed at Holly. Cowboy bolted down the road and Holly's horse followed quickly behind him.

Buster took off running.

Dillon scanned the thick woods teeming with evergreen pines lining the banks of the river. He searched for Chandler, cursing he had figured the guy wrong.

The sniper was nowhere in sight, and for the moment, Dillon was pinned. He lay still, stretched out along a natural contour of the land, his ears tuned for any sound. A dragonfly flitted by and landed on a blooming weed, its wings fluttering in the sunlight. In the river, a turtle that had earlier slid off the log it was sunning on floated to the surface and poked its head above the water.

Dillon mopped a bead of sweat that had trickled down the side of his face and wiped his damp palm on the side of his pants. He tossed a stick into the bushes hoping to draw out the shooter.

It was hot and Dillon's mouth was dry. He picked up a smooth pebble, brushed off the dirt, and put it under his tongue to wet his mouth.

"I'm sorry that had to happen."

Dillon catapulted up and leaned into the tree for cover, swinging his AK in the direction of the voice.

"Whoa," Chandler said, walking up to the tree concealing Dillon. "I'm on your side. I'm not going to shoot. If I had planned to kill you I already would have. You're wanted dead or alive and dead would be much easier."

"How do I know you're telling the truth?" Dillon asked.

"I don't lie." Chandler's face showed no emotion.

Dillon held Chandler's piercing stare and studied his body for any indication he was lying. Standing close, he watched for fast blinking, nervous scratching, hands covering the face, or even uneven breathing, all signs he had seen in the courtroom when a defendant lied.

"That's honest enough," Dillon said. Rising from his crouched position, he emerged from around the tree, still holding the AK in a firing position. "If you go for that rifle, I'll put a slug right through your heart. And nobody is taking me or Holly in."

"Fair enough," Chandler said. He extended a hand to Dillon, who returned a cautious handshake.

Dillon eyed him curiously. "So you don't want the reward?"

"Take money from that piece of shit Cole Cassel?" Chandler shook his head. "No way. While Frank was salivating over Holly I put myself in a position where I could get a better shot. I wasn't about to let Frank take you in and collect the bounty you and Holly have on your heads."

"Why not?"

"Plenty of reasons. One being I don't like that bastard Cole Cassel. Plus I knew what was in store for Holly, and I couldn't let that happen. The town has descended into lawless chaos, and I think the boss is letting things get out of hand, then when the time is right, he'll swoop in and save everyone."

"Interesting strategy."

"One that will probably work," Chandler said.

"Weren't you part of their group?" Dillon said.

"I was for a little while. I thought they were going to honestly patrol the county boundary. After they robbed and stole from several groups of people, I bided my time until I had a reason to get rid of them."

"Some might think that's cold-blooded murder."

"Do you?"

"No, times are different now." Dillon shook his head. "So, Chandler what's *your* story?"

Chapter 11

Chandler's gaze dropped to the ground and he pulled out a thread on his pants. "My story is pretty simple. He balled the thread and flicked it away. "I had my life all planned out. Enlist, serve a few tours, save my money, come home, get a job, get married, have kids, and live happily ever after."

"Then reality intervened," Holly said riding up to them.

"That and the fact I caught my girlfriend sleeping with my best friend."

"That couldn't have ended well," Dillon said.

"Cost me two nights in jail. Then the EMP struck and a few days later I heard there was a new sheriff who needed help keeping the county borders secure. That's how I met Cole. I didn't realize he was a murderous SOB."

"Thanks for getting my horse, Holly," Dillon said.

Holly acknowledged the thanks with a nod, dismounted her horse, and handed Cowboy's reins to Dillon. Sighting the dead men, bile rose up and burned her throat. Flies had already congregated around their glassy eyes. "Should we bury them?"

Dillon waited for Chandler's reaction.

"Nah," Chandler said. He observed the fast current and the

muddy water of the river. "Let's throw them in the river and let nature dispose of them. The catfish will be eating good for a long while."

"Remind me not to go fishing anytime soon," Holly said ruefully.

While Holly held the horses, Chandler and Dillon stripped the dead men of their weapons and ammo. Checking their pockets, Dillon found a pack of cigarettes, matches, and a few coins.

"You smoke?" Chandler asked when he saw Dillon put the cigarettes in his pocket.

"No. Keeping these as barter."

"Good idea."

Flipping open a wallet, Dillon briefly checked the driver's license, taking note of the name. He thumbed through the rest of the contents. An insurance card, card key for an office building, various membership cards, useless tokens of the world after the EMP struck. There were three twenties, which he knew were useless now, then decided what the heck, he'd keep them. He pulled out his own wallet and stuffed the twenties inside. He didn't notice when one of his membership cards, one with his picture and name on it, tumbled out and fell to the ground.

One by one, Dillon and Chandler tossed the dead men into the river without so much as a second thought. The new order of the times required a more practical approach to getting things done, and burying a body would expend too much energy.

"So," Chandler said, "mind if I tag along to wherever you are going?"

Chapter 12

Dillon wasn't sure if he wanted Chandler to accompany them because he still questioned the guy's motives.

"I figured you'd be going back to town," Dillon said.

"There's nothing there for me," Chandler said. "My friends are gone, and I'm not about to let my former girlfriend worm her way back into my life. My parents live in Central Texas, so there's not one reason to go back to town. Everything I own is in my backpack. Besides, there'd be too many questions about what happened to Frank and the other guys."

"True," Dillon agreed.

"Like I said, I don't lie. I wouldn't make a good liar. Truth is the best policy because you always remember the truth. Lies are too hard to keep track of or who you told what. As a prosecutor, you should know that."

"You're right about that. Liars can't keep their lies straight," Dillon said. "I've caught too many defendants red-handed on the stand."

"So is it okay if I tag along?"

"It's not really my place to say you can or can't. It's Holly's place we're going back to."

"Ma'am," Chandler said, "what do you think? I grew up hunting and fishing, and working my grandpa's garden. I know how to grow vegetables, till the soil. I can shoot, and it would be a pleasure to work for you."

"I can't pay you," Holly stated.

"I don't need to get paid, ma'am. I'll do an honest day's work if you feed me and let me hang my hat somewhere. I'll even sleep in the barn."

Holly sensed his sincerity and his need to belong. In this new world without friends or family, a loner wouldn't last long.

"Okay, on one condition," Holly said. "You can stop calling me *ma'am*." She sighed. "It makes me feel old."

"Anything you say. Want me to call you Mrs. Hudson?"

"Well, you do have manners, I'll give you credit for that much. I'm not married, and calling me 'Mrs. Hudson' is nearly as bad as 'ma'am'. My mother was 'Mrs. Hudson' not me. Holly will be fine."

Dillon stifled a laugh.

"What's so funny?" Holly demanded, shooting him that *look.*

"Nothing," Dillon said, scratching his forehead. "Nothing at all."

"Thank you, Holly," Chandler said. He looped his backpack over his arms then slung his rifle over his shoulder. "I'm ready if you are. Which way is home?"

"Across the bridge then head south for about thirty miles," Holly said.

"If you walk while we ride, you'll only slow us down," Dillon said. "We're trying to get home before nightfall. Holly can ride with me and you can ride her horse."

"I think that'll work," Holly said. "Cowboy is the stronger horse, and he'll be able to carry our combined weight. I'm guessing we have about a few hours' ride to my ranch. Cowboy will be okay for that length of time." Holly dismounted her horse and gave the reins to Chandler.

"I appreciate that," Chandler said. "What's the horse's name?"

"Yeah," Dillon said. "You've never told me your horse's name either."

"Indian."

"Seriously?" Dillon asked.

"Seriously."

"As in Cowboys and Indians?"

Holly nodded.

"Why?"

Holly shrugged and reached up for Dillon's hand. He clasped his hand around her forearm and she put a foot in the stirrup. With a heave, she hoisted the other leg over the saddle, put her arms around Dillon's waist, leaned into him, and whispered, "I thought it was cute."

As Dillon was about to say the magic phrase to coax Cowboy into a trot, he realized he hadn't seen Buster in a while. "Hey, has anyone seen Buster?"

"That's your dog, right?" Chandler asked.

"Yes."

"Last I saw of him was right before I started shooting," Chandler said.

"You didn't hit him did you?"

"Of course not. I wouldn't shoot a dog. What kind of guy do you think I am?" Chandler was incredulous Dillon would even ask such a boneheaded question.

"Sorry," Dillon said. "I'm worried about Buster. He normally stays so close he's like my shadow."

"I think he took off running behind the horses when Chandler started firing," Holly said. "He was right next to us when you told us to get down. That's the last I saw of him."

"We need to find him," Dillon stated. "He must be close by somewhere. Let's split up. Chandler, you check by the river. Holly and I will check the road. Meet back here in ten minutes."

* * *

It was late afternoon.

The wind had picked up with a cool burst of air, and low clouds rimmed the horizon, bringing with it the peculiar smell of incoming rain.

The riders called for Buster among the wayward trails of pines and thickets, of silent dens where animals lay curled, safe from predators and protected from the elements. Anxious voices echoed loud along the languid river, quietly fading into the vast expanse of the East Texas tall pines and stately oaks.

The silence was deafening.

A mockingbird sitting on a low branch sent out a curious call, falling silent until a similar melody answered. A rabbit scurried in the underbrush, rustling leaves.

Dillon and Holly scanned the road, calling for Buster, waiting for him to emerge from the brush. There was no sound or sign of him, perhaps a whimper or a paw print, and it was like he had vanished into the tangle of pines and oaks.

"Where could he be?" Dillon asked. A deep furrow lined his forehead.

"He's got to be close by," Holly reassured him. She tried to sound as reassuring as she could, but even Holly was beginning to worry.

Five long minutes passed.

Then five more.

The low clouds darkened, and somewhere in the distance thunder rumbled.

"I think it's time we head back to the bridge," Holly said. "Maybe Chandler has found him."

Coming back to the bridge, Chandler was already waiting for them. Dillon scanned in every direction hoping against hope that Buster had been found. That slobbery tongue and smelly breath Dillon avoided would be welcome and once he found Buster he'd let his dog lick him all over. He'd give him an extra pat and food, and tell him he was a good boy.

From Chandler's expressionless face and slumped shoulders Dillon knew Buster hadn't been found.

"I looked everywhere," Chandler said. "I'm sorry." His eyes went to the low clouds rolling across the countryside. A crack of lightning illuminated the dark clouds. The horses tossed their heads and stamped their hooves at the ominous sounds, their instincts alerting them to the fast-moving storm.

"We can't leave him here," Dillon said, his voice cracking.

Holly put a hand on his shoulder. "Dillon, we need to find shelter. This is going to get bad, and it's going to be dark soon. We don't want to be caught out in the open."

"You and Chandler go. I'll stay here and wait for Buster."

"No, Dillon. We all have to go. We can always come back when the weather is better. Our supplies are running low. You know that."

Dillon hung his head. "I can't lose him, too. He's the only

connection I have to Cassie."

"Buster will be okay. He's a big dog and he can take care of himself." Holly inhaled a big breath and let it out slowly. "Dillon, we have to go now."

"Holly's right," Chandler said. "Let's go now, while there is still light, and when we get to Holly's ranch, we'll get more supplies, and I'll come back here with you. Deal?"

"I guess so," Dillon said.

The three travelers headed southwest, away from the dead men floating face down in the river, away from the lost dog. If Dillon had been alone, he would have stayed regardless if he had any food or supplies. He'd find a way to survive in the unforgiving environment. He'd carve a dugout somewhere and hole up until the storm passed. It pained him to leave Buster. It was like he was losing Cassie all over again, and a hollow feeling swallowed him as if he had been sucked into a black hole.

Silence was thick with melancholy hovering over them like storm clouds as they rode, casting a dull pall. The rhythmic sounds of hooves on blacktop and of creaking saddle leather were their only companions on the monotonous ride.

Onward the three went with their shoulders hunched and as Dillon studied the sky he thought of Buster, his buddy, the dog his daughter had given him.

Dillon had failed his daughter, and his dog was lost. What else could go wrong?

Chapter 13

Buster lay hidden in the thick brush, panting heavily and shivering from the unexpected thunder and lightning tendrils illuminating the dark sky.

It was silent for a few moments until another loud clap of thunder rolled over the countryside. Buster shivered at the thunderous noise. His tongue hung to the side and long strings of drool dripped from his mouth.

A cold burst of air was forced down from the thundercloud, dropping the temperature twenty degrees in a matter of a few minutes.

The wind and rain lashed the trees, bending them, cracking the weakest branches and sending them crashing to the ground.

Buster flinched at the noise.

As a hunting dog, he was accustomed to guns and the metallic clicking and pinging sounds they made, and was used to the storms of the Texas Gulf Coast.

He had many times observed his owner deftly handling pistols and rifles, racking slides back or taking them apart to clean them. The pungent odor of Hoppe's number 9 solvent was like perfume to Buster and he waited patiently by Dillon's side as he cleaned the firearms. The chemicals tickled his nose, but it wasn't an unpleasant odor, only one to associate with firearms and his owner.

Buster's keen association with firearms and comradery changed when Dillon was attacked and nearly killed by the alligator. Buster—the protector, lookout, guard, and companion—had miserably failed his owner. When he caught the fresh scent of the solvent on Chandler, Buster's demeanor changed. The stranger had approached his pack, and like a protector, Buster should have stepped in between his pack and this unknown man. Yet when it was time for Buster to do his duty, his legs quivered and he stayed back, behind Dillon where he felt safe from harm.

His eyes followed Chandler's hands to the rife he carried and he took in the unique smell of the rifle.

It had been recently cleaned, and the odor brought back unwanted memories of the helplessness of the situation when Dillon was being thrashed by the alligator in the bowels of the Atchafalaya Basin. Buster's mind took him to the blast of the AK when Holly picked it up, shooting.

The dark water had been dangerous with a strange scent, and though Buster couldn't identify the danger, his instinct had guided him to stay back where it was safe.

When the water exploded and his owner became overpowered, Buster was frozen with fear and indecision. His canine mind struggled with the decision to fight or flee, so he acted as he only knew to do. He barked, loud and raucous to sound an alarm to warn the woodland animals of the impending danger.

When Holly emerged from the woods, Buster felt a sense of relief as well as incompetence from not being able to help his owner.

In the chaotic situation, Holly had shouldered the AK, firing twice—once a practice shot, the other the fatal shot.

Buster associated the blasts from the AK to his failure as part of the pack, to protect it from harm regardless if it was manmade or if it came from the wild.

Holly had dragged Dillon to land and Buster cautiously approached his lifeless owner, whining and licking his hand and face, willing him to breathe. When Holly told him he was a good dog, the intonation was lost on her breathless words and the seriousness of her tone, for Buster understood life was draining from his pack leader.

Miraculously, Dillon had survived, fighting for days to regain consciousness. During that time Buster had not left his side. If he couldn't protect his owner from harm, he could at least offer comfort.

Though Buster couldn't understand the meaning of Post Traumatic Stress Syndrome, he was exhibiting the same symptoms as a soldier would, so when he heard the first rifle crack, he froze.

The flight or fight response captured him at the first rifle shot and the second one had only solidified Buster's instinct to flee, to retreat as quickly as possible from the sounds that assaulted his ears, reverberating along his body. He ran faster than the horses did, ran further down the winding road, past looming trees and dark grasses. His legs gobbled up distance until his chest and lungs hurt. When there was no more reason to run he stopped, expecting Holly and her horse to be behind him.

Confusion gripped Buster as he apprehensively checked the area around him. His nostrils flared at the smells of the new environment. A raccoon had scurried along the curve of the road, an armadillo had burrowed under a fallen tree, a bird whistled a strange melody. Something rustled the leaves and Buster twitched nervously at the sounds, actions unbecoming a dog of his stature.

The rain came, pelting him with silver dollar droplets of cold rain, soaking his coat. Buster shivered in the waning light until darkness fell and the storm rolled past.

During the long and cold night, he slept fitfully on the damp leaves, smelling of the woodland rain and creatures who had slept there before him.

At daybreak, he rose and stretched, his stomach growling from hunger and thirst. Instinct guided him to drink muddy water from a ditch, lapping it until his belly was full.

He tucked his tail and trotted slowly at first along the road, then faster as he ran past abandoned trucks and pastures of cows. The scent of the river gradually lessoned until it was only a fleeting memory, and when Buster stopped he found himself lost in the woods, away from his pack, away from safety.

Chapter 14

Garrett was standing next to the truck they had taken out of the garage.

"Hey, Ryan, get James and Cassie, and let's head into town before this truck quits on us. There's a store on the town square that has equipment that you'll need."

Ryan stepped closer to Garrett. "Would it be possible for you to drive us a little further, closer to Hemphill?"

"That's only a few miles across the state line, right?"

"Yes."

"I suppose so." Garrett scratched the side of his head. "What's in Hemphill?"

"I know someone who can help us."

"Who?"

Ryan shook his head. "I only know the name. Probably nobody you know. My parents told me that if I ever needed help I could count on them."

Garrett shrugged. "I wish you luck with that."

"I appreciate that you're helping us," Ryan said. "When this EMP thing is over—"

"Son," Garrett interrupted, "it's never going to be over. Things will never get back to the way they were. From what I've read, this is only the beginning. Society is about to change. You don't need to worry, you don't owe me anything. It's been a real honor to be able to help out the daughter of the man who is prosecuting Cole Cassel."

"I'm sorry about what happened to your son."

"I know. Sometimes I wish me and my wife had had a bunch of kids. She wasn't able to." Garrett got a faraway look in his eyes. "Thankfully I still have my grandson and my daughter-in-law." He paused, then looked pointedly at Ryan. "Why are you helping Cassie? You could have parted ways and told her good luck. What stopped you?"

"I promised Cassie I'd take her back to Houston where her dad is. She's counting on me, and I always keep my promises. Besides, I'm hoping when we get to Hemphill, we can rest and get more supplies."

"You could stay here. The offer is open if you change your mind."

"You've already done enough for us. We've got a change of clothes, our bellies are full, and…you saved our lives."

"And you saved my dog. My son's dog." Changing the subject, he said, "I don't mean to pry, but how long have you known Cassie?"

"We met on the airplane."

"You like that girl, don't you?"

"I do. I wish I could have met her under different circumstances, but I can tell you that I've learned a lot about her over these past few days. She's got grit, that's for sure. She's smart, and I know she's worried about her father. She said her father must be going out of his mind worrying about her."

"A parent never stops worrying about their kids, even if they're grown. What about your parents, Ryan? I haven't heard you talk about them."

"They are deceased. They were old when I was adopted. They were adamant about me going to Hemphill if I ever got into trouble."

"Hmm." Garrett rubbed the stubble on his chin. "Where are your birth parents from? You don't suppose—"

"—that they are from Hemphill?"

"Right."

"I have no clue. I asked to see my birth certificate, but it had been tampered with. I don't know who my birth parents are."

"Sorry to hear that. A man needs to know where he is from. What stock he descends from. But knowing you for only a little while, and seeing how you saved Gumbo, you'll do fine, son. Be true to yourself, the Almighty, family, and stick close to Cassie. I like her too. And carry a big gun. Remember: faith, family, and—"

"—firearms. I remember."

* * *

After Garrett got the truck running, he drove Cassie, Ryan, and James into town.

Cassie was sandwiched between Garrett and Ryan, while James rode in the back. The cramped cab didn't afford any extra leg or shoulder room and it was impossible not to touch Ryan. At first it felt weird with their legs touching, but as time passed, Cassie grew more comfortable. She was sure he must be feeling the same because when his hand landed on her thigh, he didn't immediately remove it.

"Sorry," he said.

"Don't worry about it," Cassie replied.

Driving along the back roads, the number of abandoned cars only reinforced the theory of an EMP attack. They only saw one other car on the road, a 1960s aqua blue Thunderbird with a recent paint job that was as shiny as a brand-spanking new car.

Garrett's truck might as well been stitched together by Frankenstein using parts found at an abandoned dump. Regardless, it ran, and when the Thunderbird passed, Garrett gave a nonchalant wave of his hand to the other driver. They both gave each other a deer in the headlights look as if they'd never seen a working car before.

"I'll stop by the local dry goods store that has clothes and some camping equipment. I think you'll need it on the road," Garrett said. "I'll see if there are any guns for sale. I can probably get you across the border and close to where you need to go, but I'll have to allow time to get back before it gets dark. It wouldn't be good to be alone after dark." Garrett glanced at Ryan. "People would kill for this truck."

"Garrett, I want you to know how thankful we are that you

helped us," Cassie said. "I don't know how I can ever repay you."

"The only payment I want is for you to get home safe. You stay with Ryan and James. They're good men, I can tell."

When Garrett drove into town, people gawked at the truck. A man ran out into the street and tried to flag them down, but Garrett sped away.

"What do you think he wanted?" Ryan asked. He looked back at the man who could only watch dejectedly as the truck rounded a corner, out of sight.

"Right now this old piece of junk would go for a million dollars." Garrett said. "But if someone wants it bad enough, they'll kill me and take it."

Garrett drove to the town square where the bank was located, along with the sundry tourist shops, the main café, a hardware store, a liquor store, and the dry goods store. The amount of broken windows was worrisome. Several stores had been looted, shelves knocked over, and Cassie gasped when a looter nonchalantly walked out of the hardware store carrying several bags.

"If looting is taking place this soon after the EMP in a country town like this, I can't imagine what it's like in a big city," Garrett said. He swung the truck into a parking space. Reaching under the seat, he retrieved a crowbar and handed it to Ryan. "If anyone tries to take it, you show this to them. Understand?"

"Yes," Ryan said.

"You have one for me?" Cassie asked. "I feel kinda naked without a weapon." She poked Ryan in the side.

"If I did, I'd give you one," Garrett said. He didn't catch the underlying meaning of Cassie's statement, but Ryan did. "I'll only be a few minutes."

Exiting the truck, Garrett let his eyes roam over the store, checking for any movement.

"See anybody in there?" Cassie asked.

"No, but since it's the only store that hasn't been broken into yet, I'm guessing Bob is in there ready to pump lead into anyone who tries."

"Be careful," Cassie urged.

"Don't worry, me and Bob go way back. Way longer than I care to remember."

"How are you going to pay him?" Ryan asked. "I don't have any money."

"Not needed. Like I said, you saved my dog, and Cassie here is Dillon's daughter."

"On second thought," Ryan said, "I'll check out the store with you."

"Me too," Cassie chimed in.

"And me," James said. "Think the truck will be okay?"

Garrett patted his pocket. "Yes. I've got the keys."

* * *

Garrett went to the store front, knocked on the door, and waited.

Bob, the store owner, unlocked the door. "Hi, Garrett, how are you?" he asked.

"Good. Thanks for letting us in," Garrett said. "I had an idea you'd be here."

"Me and Smith and Wesson," Bob said. He opened up one side of his vest."

Garrett nodded his approval. "We don't have much time. These folks need to be outfitted for survival equipment."

"Come in, come in," Bob urged. "You're at the right place."

Garrett and the rest strode into the store. Bob shut and locked the door, but in his haste didn't realize the lock didn't engage. "It's good to see a familiar face," he said. "I've been camping out for several days after looters got the store next to me. People are desperate."

"I know," Garrett said.

"Help yourself. I'll be at the counter if you need anything."

The ragged bunch perused the store selecting items they needed such as waterproof matches, a magnesium firestarter, nesting cook pot set, Nalgene bottle, LifeStraw, a knife, campware and plates, freeze dried meals, flashlights and batteries, a compass, and a map. Ryan also grabbed a tarp, mosquito repellant, duct tape, and paracord. In a pinch, he could tie the paracord around trees and drape the tarp over it for a quick shelter.

The group quickly grabbed bottled water, a change of clothes each, and eyeballed the boots. On the way to the dressing room, Cassie snatched a pack of baby wipes for future use.

Ten minutes later, Garrett walked into the dressing room where

Cassie, Ryan, and James were trying on their new clothes.

"Y'all suited up?"

"I'll be ready in a minute," Cassie said.

"Get what you need 'cause we're leavin' in five minutes. I'm going to grab a Ruger 10-22 and several boxes of ammo. I'll get Cassie something that will fit her hands. Meet me out front in five minutes." Garrett clapped his hands twice in quick succession. "Get on it. I'm going to settle the bill."

James had already packed his backpack and had hurried through the swinging doors with Garrett, leaving Cassie and Ryan alone.

"I feel better already," Ryan said. "We're so lucky to have stumbled upon him."

"I know," Cassie said. "Having a bath and clean clothes makes a girl feel good." Cassie leaned up against a wall in the dressing room. Days of walking and lack of sleep had finally caught up with her. "I'm ready to be home."

"I know you are," Ryan said. "Only a few more days and we'll be there." He looped the new backpack through his arms and heaved it over his back. "I'll get you to your dad. I promise." He reached up to Cassie's face and brushed an errant hair away.

For a moment Cassie held his gaze, acutely aware of how close he was to her.

It was muggy in the dressing room from the lack of AC, that and the fact she had on long pants caused the heat in her cheeks to rise. Garrett's and James' muffled voices carried along the racks of clothes and sundry camping equipment. She closed her eyes, her thoughts taking her back to behind the pump house at Garrett's house. A grin broke across her face. She'd caught Ryan staring at her as she stood naked, bathing. If only it was a different time, a different place, they might—

A volley of bullets struck the store, splintering wood and ricocheting off metal.

Garrett swiveled around, searching for the intruder. He crouched and returned fire.

Bob ducked behind the cash register and returned fire.

Ryan threw Cassie to the ground. He shrugged off his backpack, unzipped it, and felt around for the rock hammer he had packed at the last minute. One end was blunt like a regular hammer, the other side a sharpened pick that could smash the hardest granite.

"Cassie, hide," he ordered.

"Where?" Cassie whispered. "There's no way out of here."

"Then stay behind me."

"What are you doing?"

"Shhh!"

Ryan crawled on his hands and knees to the swinging doors leading out into the store. He lowered his head to the floor and peeked around the doors trying to see who was shooting at them. Another volley of bullets peppered the store and he instinctively flinched and withdrew.

It was quiet for a few moments until heavy footfalls upon the floor pounded closer to the dressing room.

Rising, Ryan held the rock hammer above his head, keeping a firm grip on the rubber handle, the steel end pointed outward.

The doors burst open and a man burst through. He stopped when he saw Cassie.

Flush up against the wall, Ryan took only a second to gauge that this man meant trouble. The wild-eyed desperate man pointed the rifle directly at Cassie.

Using all his strength, Ryan slammed the rock hammer into the back of the man's skull, crushing it with a wicked blow. A burst of gunfire peppered the wall above Cassie. She ducked and covered her head.

The man stumbled backward, dazed at the blow. Still he refused to fall. He fumbled with the rifle, readying it to shoot.

Ryan held up the rock hammer as if he was a major leaguer preparing to swing a bat to hit a homerun. Rushing the man, he heaved the hammer at the man's skull and pummeled his brain.

The man grunted at the force of bone breaking and splintering. He crumpled to the floor, yet refused to relinquish his rifle.

Ryan repeatedly struck him with the hammer, and when the point broke, Ryan flipped it over and pummeled him with the flat side.

The rifle fell out of the man's hand onto the floor and Ryan kicked it away.

Finally the man lay still.

Ryan stepped back and leaned against a wall. Sweat beaded his forehead and he brushed it away with the back of his hand. His heart was beating at breakneck speed, and he breathed fast and hard.

Cassie's eyes were wide and she trembled, holding on the rifle so hard her knuckles were white. She had the rifle butt secured against her shoulder, left hand on the stock, index finger ready to shoot if necessary.

"All I do is pull the trigger, right?" Her voice was shaky.

Ryan swallowed hard and let out a big breath. "Yeah," he said. "I think he's dead, so you're good."

"What do I do?"

"Stay there a moment while I get my wits about myself."

Garrett burst into the dressing room and took a quick sweep of the close quarters. Cassie sat huddled in the corner, holding the rifle. Ryan was leaning up against the wall, his fingers clutched tightly around the rock hammer. His shirt was splattered with blood.

"Is anybody shot?" His question was met with blank stares. His gaze swiveled from Cassie to Ryan. He raised his voice and repeated with definite anxiety, "Is anybody shot?"

"No. We're okay. He's not, though." Ryan pointed to the dead man on the floor.

"Sure about that?"

"Sure as the sun rises in the morning."

Taking a glance at Ryan's bloody shirt, Garrett said, "Grab a new shirt and let's get out of here."

"What about you?" Cassie asked. She motioned to his arm. "You're bleeding."

"It's nothing. A scrape. Don't worry about it." His words were stunted and breathless. "Let's go. Now!" Garrett hooked an arm under Cassie and lifted her up. He quickly pivoted and went to the dead man, rummaging through the dead man's pockets. Finding an extra clip, he tossed it to Cassie. "You'll need this."

On the way out of the store, Ryan grabbed a clean shirt. The three sprinted to the old truck, scrambled in, Garrett in the driver's seat, Cassie and Ryan next to him.

"Wait!" Cassie shouted. "We forgot James."

"No we didn't," Garrett said. He put the truck in gear, revved the engine, and peeled out, spraying the sidewalk with rocks and pebbles. The truck fish-tailed as it gained traction.

"James is dead?" Cassie squeaked. She glanced back at the store. "You're leaving him there?"

"Miss," Garrett said exasperated, "We got shot at, your

boyfriend—"

"He's not my boyfriend."

"—saved your pretty little ass by clubbing that man to death. If he hadn't been there to save you, you'd probably be spread out dead on the floor." Garrett checked the review mirror in case anyone was following them. Garrett swung the truck to the left and cut across the median, dodging stalled cars.

"I still can't believe you left him there. He helped us. He fixed your truck, so without him, we'd still be back at your house."

Ryan put a hand on Cassie's arm. "Don't," he whispered. "Let it go."

"I may be old," Garrett said gruffly, "but my hearing still works. Missy, once a person is dead there's nothing else you can do for them. Funerals are for the living, not the dead. The dead don't care what happens to their body. They're gone. Forever. What'd you want me to do? Take him to the local funeral parlor so his blood can be drained, replaced by formaldehyde or whatever unnatural liquid they use to preserve a body, and have him stuffed in some rickety coffin? This is the new way of life, so you'd better get used to it."

"What happened to Bob?" Cassie asked.

"He's okay. I'll drive you and Ryan as far as I can, and I'll come back and check on Bob. Satisfied?"

Cassie said nothing, realizing this new world was more terrifying than anything she had ever experienced.

.

Chapter 15

"Chandler, how did Cole Cassel take over the county so quickly?" Dillon asked after they had ridden for some time in silence.

Chandler quickly caught up with Dillon and Holly. "Talk was he killed the sheriff, stole his guns, and single-handedly took over the sheriff's office. There were two deputies he somehow convinced to be part of the new law.

"I was in town when he called a meeting on the town square where he laid out the way things were going to be. He was already backed up by the two deputies, along with about ten local ranchers who had already been accosted by travelers. Cole said he would close the county and not let anybody in unless they could prove they lived here. If anyone wanted to pass through, they had to pay a hefty toll.

"I heard a couple of his groupies tried to collect tolls from residents of the county, but that didn't go over too well."

Dillon recalled the run-in he had with one of Cole's earlier deputies when he rode Cowboy into town when he needed antibiotics for Holly. Better to let sleeping dogs lie. Better yet, let dead men stay dead where they had been rolled into a ditch.

Trees swayed and long grass waved as if trying to outrun the storm. Dark and ominous thunderclouds billowed into the late afternoon sky. A crack of lightning followed by rumbling thunder rolled across the land. A sprinkling of rain fell, then droplets as big as silver dollars fell upon the riders.

"I think we better find cover," Chandler said.

"We're only about ten miles from my house," Holly said, raising her voice over the storm rolling in. "Don't you think we can make it?" She was so cold she was having trouble enunciating words clearly. A shiver captured her and she pulled closer to Dillon, trying to warm up.

"We need to find shelter or we're all going to get hypothermic," Dillon said. "Horses need rest too."

He scanned the horizon, past the trees, past the empty roads and dark woods. Blinking through the rain, he detected a flicker of light in the distance.

"There's a house up ahead!" he called. "Let's stop there for a little while until the storm lets up."

The three travelers encouraged their horses to pick up the pace.

It was raining heavily now, soaking everyone to the bone. Holly shivered from the cold rain, thinking she'd never be warm again.

Coming around a relaxed bend in the road, the travelers stopped.

A bolt of lightning illuminated the ranch house set off from the road. The two-story house was dark and appeared vacant, yet Dillon swore he had seen a light moments earlier. Stopping and asking for shelter at this dark hour could lead to trouble.

"Holly," Dillon said, "by any chance do you know who lives there?"

"I think so."

"Finally some luck," Dillon mumbled. "Friend or foe?"

"Not sure," Holly said, aware of the risk they were taking. "It depends on if the guy is still alive or not."

Chapter 16

"That's close enough," a male voice called out from the dark house.

Dillon and Chandler pulled in the reins of their horses. The two men exchanged wary glances, their shoulders hunched from the rain pelting them. Holly held her arms tight around Dillon, peeking out from behind him. Another crack of lightning illuminated the house in blasts of flashing yellow lights like a strobe at a disco.

"I've got a twelve gauge shotgun trained square on your chest, so if you try anything funny, I'll blow a hole big as Montana in all of you, including the woman. I don't discriminate."

"That's nice to know," Holly whispered.

"Quiet, let me do the talking." Turning his attention back to the house, he yelled, "We only need to stay a few hours until the storm lets up, that's all!" He scanned the windows and doors of the house trying to find where the man was hiding. It was as dark as the night. "Maybe we could take shelter in your barn?"

"You'd better leave," the man ordered. "I don't like strangers coming up to my house at night."

"We don't mean any harm. We only want to get out of this lightning storm and get our horses—"

A flash of lightning followed by an ear-splitting crack of thunder caused Dillon to automatically flinch and hunch over. Cowboy tossed his head and stamped his hooves at the thunderous noise. There was a brief interlude followed by intense lightning. Dillon struggled to calm Cowboy as the storm intensified.

Holly raised an arm and waved. "I'm Holly Hudson and I own a ranch about ten miles south of here."

"What'd you say your name was?" the man yelled.

"Holly Hudson. Do you remember me?"

"Are you Nick's daughter?" A door squeaked open and the man peered around from the door. A beam of light cast out into the dark night.

"Yes! I'm Nick and Brenda's daughter."

"Well, I'll be!" The man stepped out of the door and onto the slatted board of the front porch. He had on a dark slicker with the hood pulled up over his head. He held the shotgun in one hand and a lantern in the other. "We used to play bridge together. Your daddy sure was competitive. Come on in out of the rain," he said. He fiddled with the lantern, casting light on the riders and their horses. "Put the horses in the barn. You'll find feed in there too."

"I'll do it," Chandler said before Dillon could offer. "You and Holly go on in and dry off."

"Thanks," Dillon said.

"You'll catch your death of cold if you don't get out of that rain. It'll suck the life right out of you."

Chandler took the horses to the barn, while Dillon and Holly, hurried up the stairs of the porch. They stepped in and took in the surroundings. The house was surprisingly warm, and the yellow glow of lanterns illuminated the living area. The aroma of meat stew filled the air. A cute dog came up to Holly, running its nose along her boots and her leg, taking in the smell of this new person.

"That's Nipper," the man said, putting on another log. He poked the embers in the fireplace then set the screen back into place. "He's my daughter's dog. Take your boots off and put them here by the fireplace."

Holly and Dillon took off their wet socks and boots. They tiptoed across the rugs covering the wood floors, and set their boots next to the fireplace.

"Sorry, I forgot to introduce myself. I'm Jack Hardy," he said glancing from Dillon to Holly. He briskly rubbed his hands together then offered a handshake.

"Dillon Stockdale."

"Nice to meet you," Jack said. "Who's your other friend?"

"Chris Chandler."

"God, it's so good to see a familiar face," Jack said, "even if I haven't seen you since you were a teenager. Let me see you, Holly." An expression of fatherly love came over Jack. He stood in front of Holly and put his hands on her shoulders. "You sure do resemble your mother."

"Thank you," Holly said.

"Amanda!" Jack screamed up the stairs. "Come on down. It's okay, these folks are neighbors!"

A young woman, hardly past being what some would call a girl, padded down the stairs. Her long hair flowed over her shoulders, and her brown eyes bounced from Holly to Dillon. The young woman had on a pair of jeans and an oversized checkered woolen shirt. She ran over to Jack.

"This is my granddaughter. Amanda, say hello to these nice folks," Jack said. He coughed a phlegm-filled cough, deep and raspy. Reaching around to his back pocket, he retrieved a handkerchief and coughed into it.

Holly and Dillon exchanged worried looks.

"Grandpa," Amanda said, concern etching her face. "Are you okay? Can I get you anything? A glass of water?"

"No, no. I'll be okay in a minute." He swallowed audibly. "Let me sit down until this subsides." Jack stepped over to a rocking chair near the fireplace and lowered himself into the chair. Coughing again, he covered his mouth with the handkerchief. "Sorry y'all had to see that. I'm not a well man."

Nipper jumped up into Jack's lap and licked his face, trying to comfort him. For a while it helped until Jack had another coughing fit.

"It's bad," Jack said. "You might as well know. Stage four lung cancer."

"Grandpa, don't," Amanda said. She put a hand to her mouth, trying to conceal the emotions boiling up inside her.

Dillon expected Amanda to burst out crying at any moment.

"Jack," Holly said, "do you have anything for your cough?"

He shook his head. "My prescription was running out, and those damned insurance companies wouldn't refill my medicine until the thirtieth day. Then the damn electricity went off and nothing works now, not even the damn truck."

"Don't cuss, Grandpa," Amanda scolded.

"Sorry," he said.

"Got any whiskey and honey?" Holly asked.

"Yes. Why?"

"I'm going to make you something that will help your cough," Holly said. "Amanda, come with me to the kitchen."

"The whiskey is in the cabinet above the refrigerator," Jack said. "And the lantern is on the counter to the left right as you walk in."

Holly followed Amanda to the kitchen. Feeling around the place, Amanda located their kerosene lantern and switched it on. Holly retrieved the whiskey from the cupboard, and taking a quick glance at the counters, she spotted the honey. "You have a lemon by any chance?"

"We do. They're in the barn. My grandpa said they'd keep longer in the cool air. I'll get you one."

"Okay, be careful. Take the lantern."

Amanda went out the back door and bolted to the barn. She covered her head with a shawl, trying not to get wet, while dangling the lantern to light her way. The storm's intensity had increased and the rain was now blowing sideways. A clap of thunder rolled over the countryside, startling Amanda. She burst through the side door of the barn, but the previous thunder wasn't nearly as jolting as seeing a man in the barn.

"Who...who are you?" she stuttered. "What are you doing here?" For a moment Amanda thought about getting a pitchfork to protect herself with, but it was obvious she was no match for the man. He was tall and burly, with a couple of weeks' worth of stubble. He wore a pair of dark washed blue-jeans and a black slicker.

"Name's Chris Chandler. Everyone calls me Chandler." He set down the bucket of feed. "I'm here with Holly and Dillon. They asked me to put the horses up and feed them."

"Oh."

"Didn't anyone tell you I was in the barn?" Chandler asked.

"No."

"What's your name?"

"Amanda Hardy."

"How old are you?" Chandler asked.

"None of your business," Amanda said.

Chandler took a curious step forward. His gaze tracked from her boots back up to her dark eyes. The wisp of a girl with long wavy hair, who probably wasn't more than five foot three, held steady and eyed him as if she was challenging him.

"You can't be more than sixteen."

"I am not!" Amanda exclaimed indignantly. "I turned twenty-one last month." She put an annoyed hand on her hip.

A slight grin spread across Chandler's face which didn't go unnoticed.

"So how old are you?" Amanda asked. "Thirty-five?"

"No, I'm twenty-eight, but sometimes I feel twice as old." There was sorrow in his voice and his chiseled features sagged. "War does that to a guy."

"Sorry, I didn't mean anything by it. You don't really look that old."

For a few long, uncomfortable moments neither one said anything. Finally, Chandler asked, "Do you need something?"

"A lemon from the bucket behind you," Amanda replied.

Chandler picked up a lemon, tossed it in the air a couple of times like a tennis ball, then pitched it to her.

Amanda deftly caught it with one hand.

"I'm impressed," Chandler said.

Making direct eye contact with him, Amanda said, "I am too."

Chapter 17

Amanda leaned against the kitchen counter while Holly whipped up an elixir of lemon juice, honey, and whiskey in a stainless steel pan.

"Won't that burn on the wood stove?" Amanda asked. She was curious regarding how Holly planned to heat it up.

"No," Holly said. "It won't come in contact with the flames, so you can use anything you normally use on a gas or electric stove. Otherwise, it's best to use cast iron."

"Is my grandpa supposed to drink all that?" Amanda asked.

"No," Holly said. "I'm making enough in case anybody wants a nightcap. I think we could all use something to keep us warm tonight and to take off the edge."

Taking it to the wood stove in the middle of the front room, Holly placed it on the heated surface and put a lid on the pan so it would heat quicker. After a few minutes it was steaming. She splashed a couple of ounces into a sturdy lowball glass.

"Here, drink this," she said, handing the drink to Jack Hardy. "It should help your cough. Be careful, it's hot."

The old man hands shook as he reached out to take the cup. "Thank you."

"Sip it a little at a time," Holly instructed. "It will soothe your throat."

Jack took a sip. "It's good," he said, stifling a cough. "I think I'll have another dose."

* * *

The men sat around the antique dining room table that had been in the family for a hundred years. The large mahogany table sat six people. Holly offered everyone a hot toddy, regardless of whether they had a cough or not. When Chandler came in, he said he could use one. Even though Holly wasn't sure if Amanda was old enough to drink, she offered a drink to her.

Amanda tasted it. "I've had these before. My mom used to give this to me when I was a little kid and got sick. It was always real treat and the best part of being sick," Amanda said. "And it put me right to sleep."

"Smart parents," Holly laughed.

"Amanda," Jack said, "come sit at the table. While you were in the barn, Dillon has been telling me what's going on. You need to hear this."

Dillon explained the EMP and the effects of it taking down the entire electrical grid, saying that anything with a computer board was useless. Different theories were discussed regarding who could be responsible, with the best guess being China or Iran.

Amanda's eyes got round as saucers as she sat dumbfounded. "You're trying to tell me that my cell phone and the internet won't be working for years?"

"Yes," Dillon answered.

"I don't believe it," Amanda shot back. "It's not possible."

"It *is* possible because it happened."

"How am I supposed to contact my teachers at college to tell them I can't be in class?"

"Education is not on the short list of things that matter right now," Dillon said. "What matters is that we live through this. If society recovers, you can go back to school."

"I'm confused about something," Jack said. "Why don't you think they nuked us instead?"

"Probably not enough nuclear warheads to do enough damage to take out the entire United States," Dillon said. "This way, nature will do all the dirty work because within a year most people, especially those in the cities, will either starve to death, kill each other off, or die of sickness."

"Like me," Jack said solemnly. He lowered his head and stared at his drink. He traced the top edge of the glass with his fingers. Feeling a cough coming on, he pulled out a hankie from his back pocket and put it to his mouth.

The atmosphere immediately became quiet and somber. Holly's gaze swiveled from Dillon then to Chandler, who both had their heads down. They were breathing quietly, being as still as possible as if they didn't want to make any noise or draw attention to themselves.

The fireplace crackled and logs shifted. Outside, the trees bent and swayed when a gust of wind and rain lashed the land. Lightning crackled and a shock of light flashed in the sky, casting eerie shadows.

Dillon peered out the window and thought he saw movement where none should be, then chalked it up to the wind lashing the trees.

"Grandpa," Amanda said, her voice cracking, "don't talk like that. You're all I have." She choked back tears and swallowed audibly.

"It's the truth," Jack snapped. "I wouldn't have had long to live anyway. The EMP is simply speeding things up. I've only been hanging on for your sake, Amanda. Look at me."

Amanda met his eyes, and while she had a difficult time holding back her emotions, she was determined not to cry in front of strangers.

"You're not a child anymore," Jack said. "You're all grown up now and have become a young woman your mom and dad would have been proud of."

"What, Grandpa? What are you saying?" Amanda blinked away the tears clouding her vision.

"Sweetie, I need you to be strong now and be the grown-up I know you can be. These past few years after your mama and daddy passed away, I've tried to teach you to be self-reliant. I've taught you how to hunt and fish, how to can vegetables, how to manage your money…" Another coughing fit rendered him unable to speak.

He took another sip of the whiskey and lemon juice elixir.

"No, Grandpa, nooo!" Amanda wailed. Abruptly, she pushed back in her chair and ran to her bedroom, away from the harsh truth, slamming a door behind her. An anguished, muffled cry intensified the already somber tone of the room.

"I can go to her," Holly said.

"Let her be," Jack said. "I'll go talk to her in a bit."

Rain lashed against the windows and the wind whistled down through the cracks of the old house. A tree branch broke away and clattered on the roof.

Dillon spied the high ceilings and flimsy windows of the old house, briefly thinking this was no place to take a stand. As soon as the storm blew through, they'd be on their way.

Finally, Holly said, "Jack, can I do anything for you?"

"As a matter of fact there is," Jack said. He sat up straight, squared his shoulders, and looked Holly directly in the eye. "Take my granddaughter with you, where she can be safe. I have a younger sister in Central Texas where Amanda can go. Someone would need to take her there."

Holly glanced at Dillon. He shook his head, indicating he wasn't ready to be responsible for a complete stranger. Holly squinted and returned an equally hard glare. She gave her own shake of her head indicating she didn't agree with him.

Holly reached over to Jack and put a hand on his arm. "Jack, we'd be glad to—"

"Holly!" Dillon interrupted. "We don't have enough food to take in another person."

"What are we supposed to do?" Holly shot back. "Just leave her here to who knows what? A girl alone, trying to take care of her sick grandfather?"

"Jack said he had taught her well on how to be self-sufficient," Dillon countered.

"She wouldn't last a week out here all by herself and you know that," Holly argued. "Besides, when we decided whether or not Chandler could come with us, you said it was my decision because it's my place. Not yours," she reminded him.

Dillon's shoulders dropped. He had played right into that. He had no retort. That bull-headed streak she had in the courtroom where she diminished lesser attorneys to shivering wads of Jell-O would serve her well in this new and dangerous world.

Shit.

He knew Holly was right and it was her decision to allow Chandler to come with them. But another girl? Dillon wasn't so sure about this. Chandler knew how to take care of himself, and quite frankly, they needed another gun hand if anything went down. He wasn't ready to be responsible for another person, especially one he didn't know. Dillon was about to lay out the reasons they couldn't take her when the girl's grandfather spoke first.

"Please," Jack said. "You have to take her. Anybody who finds this house will more than likely kill her. She wouldn't stand a chance. Not a young woman alone. I know my sister would take her in at her ranch near Austin. Amanda can go there if someone can take her." Jack looked at Dillon and Chandler, waiting for their reactions. "I can't offer you any money, but I do have some ammo you might need. Take it all, please. I won't need it anymore. It's in my bedroom upstairs."

"What kind of ammo?" Chandler asked.

"Lots of 9 mm."

"Jack," Chandler said, deciding, "I'll look after her. You have my word on that."

"Thank you," the old man said.

"Jack, if we do allow her to come with us, what are *you* going to do?" Holly asked.

"Die," Jack said with the same emotion as if he said he was going to do dishes. He took off his bifocals and rubbed a rheumy eye. His little dog jumped in his lap and leaned into the old man. Jack stroked all along his dog's ruff to comfort him. "Die is all there is left for me to do. I've been trying to hide how sick I've been from Amanda. I didn't want her to see me like that."

"I'm sorry," Holly said.

"Please say you'll take her, Holly. Your dad would have taken her in if I asked. And my dog too. His name is Nipper. He doesn't eat much."

Dillon groaned silently to himself. Now the old man was laying on the guilt.

Holly reached over to Jack and put a hand on his arm. Their eyes met and Holly communicated with a silent nod. Dillon and Chandler cast wary glances at each other during the sad moment. It was as quiet in the house as if they were in church bowing their heads during a silent prayer.

The silence was shattered by the crack of a rifle.

A round blew a hole through a window, slammed into Jack's forehead, and obliterated the back of his head on exit. Brain matter and bone fragments splattered onto the wall behind him. The glass he was holding rocketed out of his hand and shattered onto the fireplace hearth. Jack's lifeless body fell to the floor with a sickening thud.

Nipper bolted to the hallway leading to the bedrooms.

"Get down!" Dillon shouted.

A volley of bullets peppered the walls.

Holly dropped to the floor and scrambled under the heavy table where she curled into a little ball.

Diving to the floor, Dillon let out a grunt when a bullet nicked the top part of his ear. A minor blood vessel opened and dripped blood on his collar. Rolling over onto his back, he held his AK across his chest and scooted to a corner of the room. He leaned his back against a wall and lifted his AK to a firing positing, aiming it squarely at the front door, ready to blast anyone coming through the entrance.

Chandler had already hit the floor and scurried for cover next to the large mahogany buffet table. He readied his semi-automatic sniper rifle, and made sure his Glock was in its holster. A backup gun was always a good thing.

A round blasted the mirror above Chandler, raining broken shards of glass down on him.

"Don't move from there," Dillon said.

"Don't plan to," Chandler said. "They're trying to flush us out into the open."

"The light," Dillon whispered. He glanced at the lantern sitting atop a coffee table. "We're sitting ducks with that on. Can anyone knock that off the table?"

"I can get to it," Holly said. She huddled under the heavy table made out of the same dark wood as the buffet.

"Don't get up," Dillon ordered. "Stay down."

Holly brought her knees up and crouched on all fours.

"Dammit! Stay down."

Holly ignored him, shifting from her stomach to her back. She grabbed hold of the heavy table legs, bent her legs at the knees, then pushed out with all her strength. A chair went flying across the wood floor. It bumped the coffee table, which caused the lamp to teeter.

For a long second the lamp wobbled from side to side.

Holly held her breath waiting for it to fall over, fearful the lamp might stay upright. Moments that seemed like hours passed, and the lamp toppled over and fell to the floor and clattered about. It rolled in Holly's direction, a smidgen out of reach of her legs. Slouching down, Chandler stuck out his leg and shoved it to her. Holly grabbed it and turned it off, sending the room into pitch blackness.

For a few tense minutes, they stayed still, letting their eyes slowly adjust to the dim light.

It was quiet until a round blew through the lock on the front door, shattering the door and the lock.

Holly flinched and covered her head with her hands.

Chandler sat motionless, peering through the sight on his rifle, the door in its crosshairs.

Dillon scanned each window cursing that the curtains were open.

"Who do you think is desperate enough to be out in this storm?" Holly whispered.

"Don't know," Chandler said, "unless one of those guys we rolled into the river miraculously lived."

"Not a chance," Dillon said.

The wind's fury lessened, as did the thunder and lightning until only the sound of rain dripping off the roof and into the gutters remained.

Dillon rose from his crouching position. "I'm going to check on—"

The shrill scream of a terrified woman, so viscerally frightened, rent the silence of the house and made the hairs on Dillon's neck stand up.

The next sound of a single gunshot and a body hitting the floor was even more terrifying.

Dillon and Chandler charged down the hallway. They bolted to Amanda's bedroom where the scream had emanated from.

What they saw took both of them by surprise.

Chapter 18

"Don't shoot, don't shoot!" Dillon said, afraid the panic stricken girl would shoot him by accident. "Put the gun down, Amanda. Everything is okay."

Despite Dillon's calming voice, Amanda was becoming more agitated by the second. She was hyperventilating and her wild eyes darted around. When Dillon asked her again to put the gun down, she didn't respond.

A large man lay face down across Amanda's legs. His arms were splayed out in front of him and a crimson stain appeared on the floor.

Dillon kicked the AK 47 away from the man.

Her eyes darted from the man to Dillon then back again. She was sitting on the floor, her back against the wall and her legs stretched out straight in front of her, pinned by the man she had shot. She clasped a Glock in her shaking hands.

Holly appeared then, standing to the side in stunned silence. Dillon cautiously approached Amanda, telling her everything would be okay. "Just give me the gun," he said in a soothing voice, as if he was her father. Reaching for the gun, he gently pried it from her hands, handing it to Holly for safekeeping.

Amanda had a blank stare on her face, as if she didn't understand a word he was saying. Her eyes dropped to the man lying across her legs. She tensed her shoulders and her eyes grew big, her whole body trembling.

"Get him off of me." She tried to wiggle her legs out from under the man but he was too heavy. "Get him off of me!" she screamed.

Dillon put his index and middle finger to the man's neck, checking for a pulse, and when he didn't find any he said, "Chandler, help me move this guy off of her."

"Is he dead?" Amanda asked.

"Yes," Dillon said.

Dillon took hold of the man's arms while Chandler took his feet. They heaved the dead guy away from Amanda, putting him face up. Dillon studied him, but couldn't place him. "Anybody know this guy?"

Holly took a quick glance at the grisly sight. She chewed on a ragged cuticle with her teeth and shook her head.

"Chandler?"

"Not sure." He took one last look at the body on the floor, then turned away.

"Come sit on the bed," Holly said to Amanda, patting the quilt. "Tell me what happened."

"I was on my bed when I heard gunshots and shouts and I didn't know what to do. I got off my bed and tried to hide." Deep wrinkles furrowed Amanda's otherwise smooth forehead. "I was so scared. I…I remembered my grandpa had put a gun in the nightstand and he told me to use it if anyone broke into the house." Rising, Amanda went to her bed and sat down next to Holly. She burst out crying. "He, he…" she sobbed, covering her face with her hands. "I heard the back door open—the one by the mud room—and when he saw me, I thought he was going to shoot me so I shot him first."

"You did the right thing," Chandler said. He patted Amanda on the shoulder.

"I think I'm going to be sick." Amanda bent over and rocked back and forth while holding her stomach.

"It takes a brave person to do what you did, Amanda. I'm proud of you," Chandler said.

The sick feeling in her stomach subsided for a moment, and she lifted her gaze. "You are?"

"Yes."

“I want my grandpa,” Amanda said. Her voice was quiet and tremulous. “Where is he?”

Dillon and Chandler glanced nervously at each other. Holly put her arms around Amanda and brought her closer.

“What’s going on?” Amanda asked. “Where’s my grandpa? Is he okay?”

“Honey,” Holly said carefully, “I’m not sure how to tell you this.”

“What?”

“I’m sorry to tell you. Your grandpa is not okay.”

“What do you mean? I don’t understand.” Amanda’s eyes darted around the room desperately. “Where is he?”

Rising off the bed, she bolted to the door. Chandler caught her before she could get any further. Holding both of her arms, he restrained her.

“Let me go!” Amanda exclaimed.

“I can’t,” Chandler said. “That man you killed, he shot your grandpa.”

“What? Is he okay?”

“He’s…no, he’s not.”

“Nooo!” Amanda wailed. “My grandpa is…no he can’t be…” Amanda searched Dillon’s and Chandler’s eyes for confirmation that her grandfather was still alive. Finding none, she burst out crying again.

“He’s gone,” Holly said gently. When she tried to comfort Amanda by putting a hand on her shoulder, Amanda recoiled. Anger rose quickly in her and she broke free from Chandler, went to the man, and kicked him in the side, hard kicks full of anger and frustration. She kicked until Chandler held her back, pinning her arms to her side. Amanda screamed at the needless loss of her grandfather, at the loss of her parents, at the loss of what she held dear to her. She crumpled in Chandler’s arms.

“Let it out,” he said. “Let it all out.”

* * *

“She’s sleeping now,” Holly said. She closed the door to Amanda’s bedroom, leaving it open a crack as Amanda had requested. Holly walked into the kitchen and took a seat at the table where Dillon and Chandler were sitting. She poured what was left of the bourbon/honey/lemon juice elixir. She downed it in one big gulp. "What did you do with the bodies?"

"We took the guy that Amanda killed and dumped him in a thicket about fifty yards from here," Dillon said. "We took Jack to the barn and wrapped him in blankets we found. We'll bury him tomorrow at first light."

"Did you know that man, Chandler?" Holly asked. She thought she had caught a brief flash of recognition in his eyes when Chandler first saw the man.

"Yeah. I didn't want to say it in front of Amanda."

"Who is he?" Dillon asked.

"I've seen him hanging around the sheriff's old office, the one that Cole Cassel took over. Said his name was Brent Hutchins. He was a loner, always staying to the side and watching people."

"Wait," Holly said. "I remember that guy now. He did some work for me a few years ago. Always gave me the creeps."

"Plus," Chandler added, "when it was time for us to meet earlier today and formulate a plan for the bridge, he was late and came up with an excuse that he couldn't help us. Frank told him Cole wouldn't be too happy about that and would probably fine him but Brent said he didn't care. I guess he changed his mind and came out to the bridge just as all the action was happening. Instead of going back into town, he probably followed us this entire time, waiting for a good time to ambush us."

"And the storm provided cover for him," Dillon said.

"Right," Chandler said. "That's why we never saw or heard him." He pulled out a folded piece of paper and slapped it on the table. "I found this in his front pocket. I guess he wanted the reward all to himself."

Dillon leaned in closer to read it.

Dillon Stockdale and Holly Hudson. Man about 45, average height, built like a running back, dark hair graying at the temples. Reward $10,000. Holly Hudson, 42, 5'6", 130 pounds, blonde hair. Reward $15,000.Wanted dead or alive.

"Right popular aren't we?" Dillon commented. He passed the flyer to Holly. "Apparently, Holly, you're more popular than I am."

"That's one popularity contest I don't want to win."

"Chandler," Dillon said, "with this bullseye on our heads I won't blame you if you want to leave. There will be no hard feelings if you do. We'll take Amanda with us and you can head on out to Central Texas where your folks are."

Chandler shook his head. "I'll stay, but under one condition."

"What's that?" Dillon asked.

"I need to know something."

"What?"

"Why does Cole Cassel have a bounty on your heads?"

Dillon explained the trial and the fact Holly was Cole's defense attorney. He went into detail about how a plane clipped the Harris County courthouse and the ensuing chaos. He explained that Cole escaped and had cornered Holly in the garage stairwell, threatening her with a knife.

"During the confrontation, I killed two of his groupies."

"I still don't understand," Chandler said. "Unless the guys you killed were two of his family members that still doesn't explain why he hates you so much."

Holly sighed. "We know each other from high school and—"

"Don't," Dillon interrupted. "You don't have to."

"I do," Holly said. She cast him a definitive stare. "Let me finish." While Holly explained their connection, that they had a child together, Chandler sat stoically, taking in the newfound knowledge.

"If I didn't win the case," Holly finished, "he said he'd kill our child."

"That's unbelievable," Chandler said.

"Believe it," Holly replied.

"The offer is still open if you want to leave," Dillon said. "We'll understand."

"When I say I'm gonna do something, I do it," Chandler said. "I'll help get Amanda to Holly's ranch, make sure you're settled, then I'll take Amanda to her great aunt's place. Besides, if Cole Cassel comes anywhere near you, Holly, or Amanda, I'll shoot him dead. Any man that would kill his own offspring to make a point needs to be deleted, and it would be my pleasure to be the one who presses the button."

"I couldn't agree with you more," Dillon said. "Well, let's try to get some rest while it's still dark. We need to bury Jack in the morning and get out of here as soon as possible. Holly and I will sleep in one of the bedrooms. Chandler, where do you plan on sleeping?”

“I’ll sleep in the hallway by Amanda’s room. If anyone else comes knocking, I’ll answer with this.” Chandler patted his rifle. “Besides, that girl has guts. I’m going to see to it that she stays safe tonight.”

Chapter 19

Cole Cassel's goal of taking over the town wasn't going as planned and he cursed the stupidity of the people in the one-horse town.

All except for Chandler.

Now that was one guy Cole respected. He had military training which came in handy, and Cole knew he should have put him in charge of the bridge instead of Frank what's-his-name. If it hadn't been for Frank's sister and the fact that she knew how to please a man, Frank would have been sent to the last of the line, no cuts allowed. She said she even had a girlfriend who'd be game for a ménage a trios. A slight smile crept across Cole's hard features at the possibility.

When the group didn't come back when they were supposed to, Cole sent Brent to check on things, and when *he* didn't come back, Cole decided to go see for himself.

After the storm passed, he peeled out of town in the truck he had stolen right after the EMP took down the electrical grid. Fifteen minutes later he crossed the bridge, parked the truck, got out, and looked around. The sky had cleared from the night's storm and the morning sun peeked over the land. The normally placid river was flowing at a swift pace and Cole scanned the muddy river on both sides. One side was steep where recent storm erosion had occurred, uprooting a tree. The other side of the river was grassy and contained a sandbar where debris from upriver had collected.

It was quiet and the place had an eerie feel about it. Cole wasn't a guy who believed in hocus pocus and the tomfoolery of magicians, and he certainly wasn't one to go visit a psychic, however, when the hair on the back of his neck stood up he took notice.

Something didn't feel right.

Cole unholstered his gun, readying for whatever had given him the willies.

Stepping off the pavement, he walked over to a tree and stood there for a moment, thinking.

It was quiet and the wind whispered lonely and long through the trees. Several buzzards glided on a hot updraft and he followed their movements.

"Hmm…"

Buzzards only circled in the sky waiting for a meal—a dead meal.

The sounds of the country magnified as Cole's imagination ran wild. He jumped at the skittering of a grasshopper, and cursed at a dove cooing. He had become a product of the city and the sounds of the city, the energy and vibe, and he was beginning to bore of this backwoods town he was in.

What he really wanted at the moment was a good stiff drink, some loud music, and a private lap dance. He forced himself to concentrate on the reason he had ventured to this isolated spot of the river.

If something had happened, it would have made sense for any conflict to be on the side of the river where he was standing, instructing travelers to pay a toll. It was the side that Frank should have protected if Frank had any sense about him, and at the moment, Cole wasn't too sure how much gray matter Frank had between his ears. He was a card shy of a full deck. Heck, he was missing several cards.

When that crazy feeling Cole had experienced earlier waned, he took out a cigarette and a box of matches from his shirt pocket, lit a smoke, and took a deep drag.

Holly and Dillon should have already been back this way,

especially after what Dorothy had told him. Dorothy had been a high school classmate of Cole's, and seeing how paranoid Cole had become, he had placed spies all around the city. One of them had seen Dillon at her house a couple of weeks ago, which had prompted a visit by Cole. Dorothy swore up and down that Dillon had shown up unexpectedly, only delivering her daughter safe and sound after an unsuccessful trip to the drugstore to find antibiotics.

Dorothy put up token resistance when Cole started rummaging around the house, and when Cole found a bottle of antibiotics, he ramped up the interrogation. Big time.

Cole put a knife to her kid's throat, telling Dorothy that if she didn't start telling the truth, he'd slice the kid's throat like it was warm butter, after which she sang like a canary. An unwanted memory flashed in Cole's mind.

When he was a kid, his mother liked canaries and had bought one for a pet. She prepared homemade food for the bird, cleaned the cage every day, and talked to it like it was a dog. The bird had even taken a liking to Cole and would perch on his shoulder when he watched TV. One night when Cole was watching TV, his father snatched the bird off of Cole's shoulder and without warning or provocation, he pulled off the bird's head and flung the twitching carcass at Cole's feet. He said he needed to teach Cole a lesson about not doing his chores. Cole's dad said he'd better clean up the feathers and bloody mess or else he'd get a whipping. The brutal incident traumatized Cole and he had never forgotten it.

But crying over dead birds was for sissies and Cole was no sissy.

Dorothy had told him Dillon and Holly were heading to Louisiana to search for Dillon's daughter, and since there was only one logical route that would take them back this way, it was obvious Dillon must have crossed here not too long ago. Unfortunately, they were now probably safe and snug back at Holly's ranch.

Cole prided himself on being able to figure people out, and one thing he never saw coming was Dillon hooking up with Holly. Didn't that beat all? The DA's number one man and the defense attorney?

Dillon had played him, that was for sure, and Cole didn't like that one bit.

He cursed himself for not commandeering enough people, but as it was, he couldn't trust anyone to stay at Holly's house to wait for them to come back.

Finishing his cigarette, he tossed it on the ground and stamped it out with the heel of his boot. For some reason, his gaze kept wandering to the debris pile on the sandbar downriver.

Needing a better look, Cole picked his way through briars and weeds along the riverbank until he came to the sandbar. He gingerly stepped on the water-soaked sand, testing the stability of it, making sure it hadn't become quicksand. Satisfied the sand could hold his weight, he strolled over to the debris pile full of tree limbs and trash.

He pulled back a few tree limbs and when he saw the body he stumbled backwards, nearly tripping over his feet.

"Jesus Christ!" he said, turning his head away in disgust, fighting to keep from throwing up.

A swarm of flies covered the body that was tangled among the pile of brush and uprooted trees. An arm poked out at an awkward angle and a mangled leg probably broken by the force of being tossed in the water against uprooted trees was also bent unnaturally. The ashen face was distorted and tobacco stained teeth were clenched together in a death grimace. A gaping hole the size of a baseball was visible on the bloodstained shirt.

Cole took a stick, swallowed hard, and poked the body. A swarm of black flies scattered into a swirling cloud. He stepped back and waved his arm, trying to thwart the flies from landing on him. He didn't want any of those maggot laying flies touching him, infesting him with God knows what disease.

He ran a hand over the stubble on his chin, wondering who the poor bastard was. It didn't take him long to figure it out. Although the dead man's jeans were wet and dirty with mud and the stink of death, Cole only knew one man who wore that brand: Frank.

Stupid son of a bitch.

Stepping away from the gruesome sight, Cole climbed back up to the bridge. Nosing around the weeds and briars, he spied empty shell casings. He picked up a couple and inspected them, suspecting they were from Chandler's high powered rifle. If they were, he sure was a turncoat.

He hocked a mouthful of angry spit on the ground. And to think he had thought highly of the guy at one time.

Man, had he been fooled. Twice! Once by Dillon, and now by Chandler.

Cole took his time searching for any other clues as to what had happened here. He found the IDs for the other two guys Cole had sent with Frank, but didn't find any shell casings from different guns, so he surmised Chandler had killed the three guys and dumped their bodies in the river, hoping the current would take care of them.

As he was about to leave, a glint caught his eye. Near a log he found a membership card poking out from a pile of leaves. Picking up the shiny card, he lifted the edge of one side of his mouth, smirking at the thumbnail print of the dark-haired man. His eyes glared at the name on the card.

Dillon Stockdale.

Cole had been right all along. That bastard Stockdale had been here, sure enough. And if he had been here, Holly would have been with him.

It was high time they paid for what they had done.

Nobody was going to make a fool out of Cole Cassel.

Nobody.

On the drive back into town, Cole formulated his plan. He'd get rid of Stockdale once and for all, and if Holly ended up as collateral damage, well so be it.

Chapter 20

"Alright," Garrett said, "this is as far as I can take you."

The hour drive from where the shootout happened at the sporting goods store to the Texas/Louisiana border had been silent. Cassie was too shell shocked to talk.

"The Sabine River is up ahead about a mile or two," Garrett said. "From there I reckon it's about fifteen miles straight into Hemphill. I'd get you closer but it's possible the bridge is being patrolled, and I can't take a chance this truck could be commandeered, even a jalopy like this. Keep to the road and if you see anyone, be careful and don't let your guard down. The backpacks you have are valuable and people will kill for them. If you walk at a steady pace and don't wear yourselves out, you should be able to make it to town by midnight."

Garrett pulled the truck to the side of the road, letting it idle. It would be getting dark soon and he was anxious to get back home to his grandson and daughter-in-law.

"We can't thank you enough," Ryan said.

"Seriously," Cassie said, "you saved our lives. We are forever indebted to you."

Garrett shook his head. "My only payment is for you two to live.

So do good by me and that's all I need. When you see your dad tell him how much I appreciate him taking the case against Cole. My son can rest in peace."

"I'll do that," Cassie said.

Exiting the truck, Cassie and Ryan stood in the road. Garrett turned the truck around using a three point turn, and right before he drove off, he leaned out the driver's side window and said, "Be careful. God be with you. And remember, faith, family, and firearms. You can't go wrong with that!"

Cassie and Ryan waved to him until Garrett's truck disappeared around the tree line.

It had been comforting listening to the whine of the engine and now that it was gone, an empty feeling washed over Cassie. The vastness of the wilderness was daunting. She was tired and ready to get where they needed to go. Twenty-four hours earlier their situation was so dire that she thought they would die. Fortunately, Garrett had found them, fed them, and equipped them, so with any luck they'd get the help they needed in Hemphill.

Cassie hitched the backpack high on her back, tugged at the straps, and joined Ryan, who was a few steps ahead of her.

Trees loomed tall on each side of the two lane road; clouds hung low in the waning light. They walked in silence, their footsteps crunching on loose pebbles, each alone in their thoughts.

Cassie's mind wandered to her dad, who must be going out of his mind by now, sitting alone at his house. She couldn't imagine how lonely he was without her mom. She let out a heavy sigh. It had been two years since her mom had died and although her dad tried to hide his feelings, she knew he was lonely. The older Cassie grew the more wise she became, and she realized her dad should have the freedom to find someone else. It wouldn't be right of her to discourage him from finding someone with whom he could share the rest of his life.

He was a good man, had a good marriage, and a lot more life to live, and while another woman would never replace her mother, Cassie was sure her dad would find someone to be his partner. If only she could let her dad know she was okay, and that she was trying to get home. At least he had Buster.

They walked for a while in silence, Cassie lagging further behind.

Ryan asked, "Do you need to rest or are you okay to keep walking?"

"I've got something in my boot," Cassie said. "Maybe my sock is bunched up or something. My foot is starting to hurt."

Ryan stopped walking and glanced around to assure himself it was safe. "Come sit over here on this log. I'll help you with your boot."

Cassie went to the log, shrugged off her backpack, and sat down. It hadn't been the best decision to break in a new pair of boots on a hike and now her feet were paying the price. Ryan set his backpack aside and knelt in front of her. He gently lifted the foot Cassie had been favoring, and put it on his knee, untied her laces, and wiggled the boot off. When he removed the sock, a pebble fell out. He picked it up and held it where Cassie could see it. "This was your problem."

"Incredible something so small can cause so much grief." Cassie reached for her sock.

"Let's rest a moment," Ryan said. "I could use a break too, and I think a foot massage would do you good."

Before Cassie could protest, Ryan had already started massaging her foot. It felt weird at first until she closed her eyes, relishing the brief reprieve from their journey. It wasn't exactly a pedicure, one she needed in the worst way, but for a wilderness pedi by the guy she had grown to like and respect, even the most expensive salon couldn't hold a candle to this.

The wind whistled through the leaves and the tangled brush of the East Texas woods. Shadows danced long on the road and a musty coolness left by the thunderstorm lingered in the air.

Somewhere a bird whistled then another in a distant tree, a woodland melody filling the air.

* * *

Buster lay hidden in the thick underbrush, exhausted from running and dodging the lightning and thunder the previous day. He slept fitfully, awakening even at the quiet sound of a twig snapping or the rustles of leaves. Unaccustomed to being alone and to the scurrying of nocturnal animals, a good night's sleep had escaped him.

He woke groggily at the sound of footsteps on the road, coming closer. Captivated by the sounds of human voices, Buster cocked his head in the direction of the group. Though he couldn't discern how many there were, it was obvious there were men, women, and children.

A child sang a song and skipped; a female voice laughed with mirth, while serious male voices dominated discussions. Intrigued by the group and guided by the empty feeling in his stomach, Buster rose and stepped away from his hiding place.

As the group passed, Buster lifted his nose taking in the odor of food grilled on an open fire lingering on their clothes. Tentatively, he stepped out of the shadows and followed the group, trotting closer until he was only a few steps behind. When one of the men turned around unexpectedly, Buster stopped, his eyes eager with hope. He thumped his tail in willing anticipation perhaps of a hopeful phrase of "come here" or "good dog," something he understood, something he craved.

He wagged his tail, waiting.

A man shouted harsh words at Buster and he flinched at the startling outburst. Unsure what to do because he had no comprehension of ill treatment, Buster cocked his head and held the intense gaze of the shouting man, who was wildly gesticulating his arms.

Confused at the odd movements, Buster's eyes darted from the man to the rest of group, waiting for a hint of what was expected of him.

A boy picked up a rock and hurled it at Buster, hitting him on his leg.

Buster yelped at the stinging sensation. His ears flopped down, his tail tucked. The boy threw a bigger rock, hitting Buster in the side. He bolted to the side of the road, away from the harsh words, away from the rocks hurled at him in anger.

Standing at the side of the road, he waited.

The man who had yelled charged Buster, running at him full force with footsteps full of anger.

Buster darted into the thick canopy of trees and vines. He dodged fallen trees and animal dens, unaware of the low branches slapping his face. Further he ran through the woods until he reached his den hidden among the saplings and undergrowth. He crawled in and sat on his haunches, panting, his eyes darting around to see if he had been followed. Trembling, he strained to listen to the sounds of the woods, searching for the harsh words among the woodland sounds.

After a while, his rapidly beating heart calmed and when it was finally silent he put his head on his paws. His hopefulness gave way to helplessness, and confused about his situation he closed his eyes and fell asleep.

The sun climbed high in the sky and fingers of steam rose from the wet canopy. The sound of woodland birds chirping filled the air and for a moment, Buster listened, his eyes following them flitting from branch to branch.

When he heard the approaching footsteps of people, he perked up his ears until he remembered the harsh words and rocks hurled at him.

He lowered his belly to the ground and put his face on his paws, the dappled shade and greenery hiding him. Strangers were to be avoided.

Laying on the damp ground, Buster listened to the travelers talk in low murmurings of people who were relaxed around each other.

The two travelers came closer and the voices comforted Buster, warming him, and he recognized the cadence of the female's voice. There was something definitely familiar about the young woman, but peering through the canopy of saplings and vines, Buster couldn't see her face clearly.

He tasted the air for a scent, but the wind had changed direction, brushing him from behind and pushing whatever knowledge he could have gained away from him.

The two, a man and a woman, stopped not far from Buster's den, and he eyed them with growing curiosity.

The woman sat down on a log and the man slid off her boot. Interested in their actions Buster rose and silently observed them.

For a long while the man massaged the woman's foot, and Buster noticed her gaze was transfixed on the man.

Intermittently, the man lifted his head and looked into the woman's eyes. They held each other's gaze for a few moments until the man lifted a hand and cradled her face. She took his hand, cupping it and closing her eyes.

Buster felt the silent connection.

The silence spoke of clear communication between the two, of the gentle handling the man showed the woman, of their relaxed postures, yet Buster sensed their troubled journey. It must have been long because the woman sat unmoving, her shoulders heavy from the burden she had been carrying.

It was a burden Buster could relate to, for he sensed the recent hunger and thirst she had experienced. Her face was reddened from exertion. He could sense her relief that the man had reached out to her, to comfort her, just as Buster needed. He needed the touch of a human being, craved it, and he couldn't understand where his owner was or his owner's companion.

There was sadness in the woman's face and when Buster crept out of his hiding place, a brief flicker of recognition captured him while his mind searched for the meaning.

With great trepidation Buster put one paw in front of the other, carefully choosing his path. His footfalls on the spongy earth were silent, catlike, and his large form melted into the shadows of the woods.

He inched closer.

The wind shifted directions and Buster lifted his nose. The scent came to him full and strong, the scent of his owner's offspring. She was the one who scratched his belly and lavished praise on him, saying "good dog"; she was the one who snuck table food to him; the one who let him sleep on her bed.

Cassie was here!

Buster leapt from the woods, a black form bursting forward in a tangled blur of flapping ears, spindly legs, and whining unbecoming to a dog of his stature.

Chapter 21

The commotion of whining and barking racing toward Ryan and Cassie caused them to rocket up and take a defensive posture.

Ryan swiveled in time to see a black projectile racing toward him with the speed of a greyhound.

The dog was massive and it was zeroing in on Cassie!

Ryan acted instinctively and drew his gun, brought it up, and sighted it on the dog. In the millisecond it took to place his index finger on the trigger, Cassie reached over and shoved his arm up. Ryan lost his balance, the gun discharged, the blast echoing into the dense canopy of trees.

A flock of redbirds scattered.

Buster stood stunned, his eyes locked on Ryan as he regained his footing.

"Ryan!" Cassie screamed. "Don't shoot!"

"That dog's rabid. Stay back."

"No!" Cassie yelled. "That's Buster."

"What?"

"Buster! The dog I gave my dad. I'm sure of it." Her words were quick and to the point. Cassie lowered her voice and in a calming tone said, "Buster, come here. Good dog. Come here, boy."

Buster swiveled his gaze from Cassie to Ryan, unsure how to proceed.

"Buster, come," Cassie said.

With tremendous joy, Buster closed the few yards standing between him and Cassie in two glorious bounds. He leapt up to Cassie, stood on his hind legs, and put his massive paws on her shoulders. He licked her face, whining and wagging his tail as if he was a puppy.

For several moments Ryan stood to the side, awestruck at the joyous reunion. Cassie fell to the ground letting Buster nuzzle and lick her until she gave the command, "Stop. That's enough." Buster acquiesced to his mistress's wishes.

"What the hell?" Ryan said. "What is your dog doing way out here? It must be over a hundred miles from here to where you live."

"I don't know what he's doing here," Cassie said standing up. She brushed off dirt and leaves from her jeans. "Maybe my dad came this way looking for me."

"Why would he think you're here?"

"I was on the phone with my dad when the plane lost electricity. I told him we had crossed the Sabine River, which meant we were descending. I guess he came to find me."

"But here?" Ryan was skeptical. "Why here? It's not the most direct route to NOLA."

"I don't know why he would come this way. It doesn't make any sense."

"Does he have any friends around here?"

"Not that I know of."

"Are you sure that's Buster?" Ryan asked.

"Of course," Cassie said. "Check his tags if you don't believe me. It's got my dad's name and phone number on it."

"I'll take your word for it. Maybe he got separated from your dad during the thunderstorm. I heard some of it last night while we were camping. Hey, is Buster scared of thunder?"

"I think he is."

"What about gunshots? Lots of dogs are gun shy."

"He could be, and if he was, it would explain why he is out here by himself. He must have run away during the thunderstorm," Cassie said. Unable to contain her enthusiasm at finding Buster, Cassie bent down and rubbed him all over. "You're a good dog. You hungry?" she asked in a tone Buster understood.

Buster sat down on his haunches, his eyes eager and his tail thumping on the ground, wiggling all over.

Cassie reached into her backpack and retrieved a piece of jerky. "Here you go," she said, handing it to the dog.

Greedily, Buster ate the jerky. Afterward, Cassie poured water into her hand and let Buster drink.

"It's a good thing we found you," Cassie said. "If only you could tell us where my dad is."

Chapter 22

"That should do it," Dillon said.

He shoveled the last bit of the East Texas red dirt on top of the freshly dug grave of Amanda's grandfather, Jack Hardy. He had scouted a location early in the morning before Amanda woke, picking a suitable spot. He chose a location not only for the ease of digging, but also a spot he thought the tough old codger would like.

It was in a clearing rimmed by tall pines where the wind and rain could come through, brushing the land, cleansing and washing it clean.

Dillon dug the grave in an east/west direction on a gently sloping declivity where the morning sun peeked through, warming the land, and where the rain could trickle away into the gully. In the hot afternoons, shade from the towering pines would protect the grave from the relentless rays. It was the least he could do for the old man.

Dillon and Chandler took turns digging and when it was as deep as they could get it, they placed Jack's body in the grave.

Fortunately the soil had been loosened by the rain the night before, and they dug until tree roots prevented further progress. It wasn't as deep as they would have liked it to be, but it should be deep enough so coyotes and other vermin couldn't dig up the body.

Earlier Dillon had washed the blood from Jack's face then placed him in a faded quilt he found in the master bedroom. With great difficulty, he put a clean shirt on the man in case Amanda wanted to view her grandfather's body so he would be presentable. Before securing the blanket, Dillon asked Amanda if she wanted to see him one last time to which she replied, "No. I want to remember him when he was alive."

Dillon had checked the old man's pockets for anything of sentimental value. Reaching deep, he found a pocket watch, and surprisingly it was still working.

Holly and Amanda joined them in time to see Dillon shovel the last mound of dirt on the grave.

Standing aside the grave, Dillon pitched the blade end of the shovel into the ground and leaned on the handle.

The rising sun heated the land, drying the dewy grass. Humidity heightened. Such was the way with Texas weather.

"Anybody want to say a few words before we lay Amanda's grandfather to rest?" Dillon swiped the back his hand across his forehead, wiping away sweat.

Amanda was weeping silently, her head bowed. She was holding her dog Nipper tight against her bosom. He was part fox terrier and part Russell terrier, and a dead ringer for the RCA Victor dog. Keeping with history, Jack had named him in honor of the famous dog.

Holly was as quiet as Dillon had ever seen her, and for a woman who made her living talking, this was totally out of character.

Chandler stepped over to Amanda and put his arm around her. She leaned her head against his chest and sobbed while he stroked her hair. "It'll be okay," he said. "We're here for you."

"Since nobody is volunteering, I'll say a few words," Dillon said. "Before I begin, Amanda, I found something I think your grandpa would've liked you to have."

"What is it?" Amanda squeaked. She swiped beneath her eyes, wiping away tears.

Reaching into his pocket, Dillon retrieved the gold plated pocket watch with a thick chain attached to it and handed it to Amanda. "I found this in your grandpa's pocket. I thought you would want it."

Amanda set Nipper down and took the pocket watch, holding it in both hands. She gazed at it lovingly. "This was a wedding present my grandmother gave him on their wedding day. My grandpa never went anywhere without it. He said even after she was gone that he would hold it and know he always had a little bit of her close to him."

"They must have loved each other very much. A love that only comes along once in a lifetime," Holly said.

Amanda dropped her head and the tears flowed easily. Dillon took her hands in his and closed them around the watch. "It's yours now."

Amanda sniffled and Chandler stepped over to her.

Dillon took a deep breath. The last funeral he had attended had been Amy's.

He cleared his throat and swallowed hard. "Dear Lord, as we gather here today let us remember the life of Jack Hardy and his Earthly years. He was a good man, husband, father, and grandfather who gave his life protecting his granddaughter. And while his body is gone from us, his soul lives on for eternity." Dillon paused before continuing in a solemn voice. "Let us bow our heads and say the Lord's Prayer together: *Our Father who art in heaven, hallowed be thy name, thy kingdom come, thy will be done, on Earth as it is in heaven. Give us this day our daily bread. Forgive us our trespasses, as we forgive those who trespass against us. And lead us not into temptation, but deliver us from evil. For thine is the kingdom, and the power, and the glory, forever and ever*. Amen."

Amanda broke away from Chandler and ran back to the house. Chandler tuned to go to her, but Holly put a hand around his arm, stopping him. "Let her go."

"She shouldn't be alone," Chandler said. "I'm afraid she might hurt herself."

"I don't think she'll do that. I talked to her this morning and reassured her that we are here for her. It seemed to make her feel better. Give her a few minutes then go to her. I think she'd like that."

Chandler glanced at Dillon. He was standing tall, wearing a working man's uniform of a pair of jeans, boots, and a shirt with the sleeves rolled up.

Dillon gave a mere nod of his head in the direction of the house, indicating it was okay to go after her.

After Chandler was out of earshot, Holly said, "I think he likes that girl."

"I think so too. She has grit. I'll give her that." It was quiet, with only the sounds of the wind on the land and the melodic chirping of a field sparrow. "You're right. We can't leave her here. She wouldn't last a month."

"I know," Holly said. "She told me she has cousins in Dallas, but that might as well be a continent away."

"She wouldn't make it there by herself anyway." Dillon took a stick and chopped away at the mud caking his boots. "We have to leave as soon as possible to get back to your ranch. I figure we'll be there by noon if we leave soon. Let's head on in and pack up. I'm eager to get going."

Dillon took Holly by the arm and led her away from the grave. They walked a few yards through the wet grass, picking their way to the road leading to the house.

In the solemn moment Dillon's thoughts went to his daughter, Cassie. He hoped that whoever found his daughter's body would treat her with the same respect with which they had treated Amanda's grandfather. The goon who killed Amanda's grandfather wasn't shown the same mercy, and Dillon was thankful that Holly hadn't asked what they had done with the guy. Leaving his body to vultures and hogs wasn't exactly civilized, yet he lost all privileges when he tried to kill them last night.

"Hey, wait a minute," Holly said. "Where's Nipper?"

"Didn't he go with Amanda?"

"No." Panic struck Holly at the possibility of another lost dog. She glanced back at the grave. Her heart sank and she put a hand to her mouth. Nipper was laying on top of the freshly dug grave, his head resting on his paws. It was as if he didn't want to abandon Amanda's grandfather.

"That's got to be the saddest thing I've ever seen," Dillon said. "He knows Jack is buried there."

"I'll go get him," Holly said, "before Amanda sees him."

* * *

After Holly coaxed Nipper away from the grave, she and Dillon walked back to the house, making sure the dog followed them.

When they came within view of the house, Nipper bolted past them and ran full speed to the front porch. He scrambled up the porch stairs, pushed open the screen door, and ran straight to Amanda's room. Dismissing Chandler, who was sitting on the edge of the bed, Nipper stood on his hind legs and nosed the bed, searching for the perfect spot to jump on. With the ease of a cat, he leapt on the bed and carefully padded over to Amanda. He nuzzled her hand with his wet nose and she placed a hand on his head. She rubbed him between his eyes then ran her fingers down the rough fur along his back. Nipper's ears flopped down and he hung his head as Amanda stroked him.

"Chandler, do you still want to come with me, to my aunt's place?" Amanda asked.

"Of course I do," the big man with a military style haircut that was in the process of growing out said softly. "I'll take care of you." He reached over to her hand and patted it.

Amanda sat up. "There's one more thing."

"What's that?"

"Nipper comes too."

Chapter 23

Ryan and Cassie walked the rest of the way to Hemphill with Buster trailing behind them. When they arrived on the outskirts of the rural town, Ryan suggested they take a break. He estimated it was around midnight, gauging the position of the constellations.

The stars twinkled among puffs of clouds floating in the inky night. As long as the moon shone, they were able to navigate the streets with relative ease, but when the sky darkened, Ryan felt uneasy.

After a brief rest, they plodded on, their footsteps heavy with fatigue as they passed darkened stores with broken windows, silent cars askew in the street. A hooded man saw them, stopped in mid-stride then melted back into the night.

Spotty gunfire erupted in the city and Ryan listened until the shots died out. He was bone tired and needed to take a quick break. He spotted an elementary school and a playground in the distance with tall trees lining the sidewalks, a motionless merry-go-round, children's swings stilled.

"Let's stop there a moment," he said motioning with his head.

"The playground?" Cassie asked.

"Yes. We can take a short break."

When they reached the school grounds, Ryan shrugged off his backpack, set it on the merry-go-round, and dug around inside. Finding a water bottle, he downed several big swallows then handed it to Cassie. She gulped water then poured a handful for Buster.

Ryan searched the outer pocket of the backpack for a map of East Texas he had swiped from the sporting goods store at the last minute. He found it, shook it open, and held it at an angle trying to utilize the glow of the waning moonlight.

"Ryan," Cassie said, her intonation indicating her annoyance and weariness, "can you now tell me the name of the people who can help us?" She shrugged out of her backpack and slung it on the ground where it landed with a loud thud. Wearily, she sat down on a bench, her shoulders hunched over.

"Sorry, I didn't mean to keep it a secret. So much has happened…it slipped my mind. Their names are Helen and Ed Reynolds. They are old friends of my parents."

"We've been together for what, a week now? And you've never even mentioned their names. When's the last time you saw them?"

"I'm not even sure I've met them. My parents always told me that if I needed help I should go to them. They made me memorize their phone number and address." Squinting at the enlarged insert street grid of Hemphill on the back of the map, he traced a line with his finger until he found the street the Reynolds lived on. "Found it!" His voice was tinged with relief and an odd feeling of

déjà vu washed over him as he stared at the street name.

He wondered if he had ever been here. It couldn't be possible, because his earliest memories were of the flat and dry land of West Texas. Surely if he had been here before he would have remembered the towering trees.

"How much further do we need to go?" Cassie asked.

"About a mile," Ryan replied.

"You seem a million miles away. What's going on?" Cassie asked.

"I'm not sure. I have a funny feeling about this place. Have you ever had that feeling of déjà vu, like you've been someplace before?"

"Every once in a while."

"I just had that. I think I've been here before because there's something really familiar about the street name."

Cassie asked, "What's the street name?"

"Mockingbird."

"Mockingbird?" Cassie repeated, flummoxed. "That's probably the most common street name in Texas. "It *is* the state bird, after all. You know that, right?"

"Maybe."

"Well, anyway, Mockingbird Lane is the most famous street in Dallas, probably all of Texas. It runs through the Highland Park area of Dallas and is a straight shot to Dallas Love Field. Who hasn't heard of that?" Cassie folded the map and handed it to Ryan.

"Me, for one. I've never been to Dallas."

"Maybe you *have* been here before."

* * *

Before they picked up their backpacks for the last mile long leg of their journey, Ryan instructed Cassie there would be no talking because he didn't want to take any chances on the last yard line of the metaphorical hundred yard dash they had made. He had seen too many football games lost when the running back's stamina ran out on the ten yard line, only to be tackled by a faster opponent.

The more they walked along Mockingbird Street, the more Ryan kept thinking he'd seen this place before. The large trees were like a canopy over the street, cloaking them in mystery, and a brief memory came back to him. He had been a toddler, perhaps three, and he was riding in the back seat of a car, captivated by the majestic grandeur of the trees. A strange shiver captured Ryan.

"You okay?" Cassie asked, picking up on his uneasiness.

"Not sure. I've got that strange feeling again."

Street numbers were painted in a large white font on each house, and as Ryan counted, a twinge of nostalgia washed over him again. He tried to shake it off, but it clung to him stubbornly. A flash of a memory playing in a front yard came to him, of a woman talking to his mother in hushed tones, glancing around as if she was concerned they were being watched.

"We're here," Ryan said. He took a deep breath and quietly walked up the walkway leading to the house, Cassie following him.

A dog barked and a slamming door from across the street caught Ryan's attention. Angry shouts of a domestic fight echoed in the night, the words indiscernible. He motioned for Cassie to stop, quieting their footsteps echoing in the lonely night.

Buster sensed the need to be quiet so he sat on his haunches, ears perked, listening.

The man who had shouted stomped angrily from the back of his house, came to his driveway and stopped dead in his tracks. He had on a dirty white muscle shirt, a pair of ill-fitting trousers, and was balding on top. He cast a wary glance at Ryan and Cassie. The man walked a few steps closer, hugging the side of his truck, took a step forward, and craned his head in Ryan's direction.

Although it was dark, it was apparent to Ryan the man was staring hard at him.

"Can I help you?" Ryan asked.

The man said nothing, and when Ryan stepped toward the direction of the man, he scurried back behind his truck and disappeared.

"That was odd," Cassie said.

"Yeah, really strange."

Coming to the front porch of the dark house, Ryan rapped his knuckles on the wood frame, jiggling the outer screen door.

He waited.

Cassie stood to the side letting her eyes roam over the neighboring houses, checking to make sure the odd man didn't reappear with a weapon.

It wasn't the best of neighborhoods. Yards hadn't been kept up and cars were parked on the front lawns. A stray dog with a tucked tail slunk around in the neighbor's yard and suspiciously eyed Buster, who returned a low growl. A rooster crowed once from the chicken coop of the neighboring house, clucking at the sight of the stray dog. Chickens made a series of throaty clicks to warn others of the possible danger.

The Reynolds' house had been better maintained than the rest of the cookie cutter houses that had been rapidly built post WWII. The porch had been recently swept and the floorboards freshly painted, although Cassie was unable to discern the exact color in the darkness. Perhaps beige. The red geraniums were in full bloom in a pot that had dark new soil sprinkled around the base of the plant. The bright yellow cushions in the rocking chair were clean.

Ryan rapped the door again, harder. He put his ear close to the door, listening for movement.

A shaky male voice from inside the house called out, "Who's there?"

"Hello," Ryan said. "My name is Ryan Manning."

"Shhh, not so loud," Cassie hissed. "Your voice travels. You'll wake the neighbors."

Ryan acknowledged Cassie's warning. He leaned into the door and spoke in a softer voice. "My name is Ryan Manning. Is this the house where Ed and Helen Reynolds live?"

"What did you say your name was?"

"Ryan—"

The front door squeaked open, letting out a sliver of light from a candle, and an old man peered through the crack. "I am Ed Reynolds and my wife is Helen."

"My name is Ryan Manning."

"I know, I heard that," Ed said. "Helen, come here. It's okay."

"Who's there, Hun?" a grandmotherly voice asked.

"It's Ryan Manning."

The white-haired woman curiously peeked from around the door, studying Ryan as if she was looking for a familiar landmark on his face.

"Ryan?" the woman said, as if she knew him. "That you?"

"Yes, ma'am. I am Ryan Manning. Do you know me?"

The woman clutched her bathrobe right around her bosom and hesitantly glanced at her husband.

"Ma'am," Ryan said, "my parents said that if I ever needed help I should come see you and your husband. They never told me why." Ryan held a hand toward Cassie. "This is my friend Cassie and her dog Bu—"

The screen door swung open and Ryan jumped back. Ed scanned the street in both directions. "Hurry, come in before anyone sees you."

Chapter 24

"*Did* anybody see you?" Ed asked quickly and with urgency.

"Your neighbor across the street did," Ryan replied. "Why? Is something wrong?"

"Probably not," Ed said, unconvincingly. "We're on edge, that's all. Come in, come in. Your dog can come in also."

Ryan and Cassie stepped into the cozy living room, furnished with a sofa, two chairs, a throw rug, framed pictures of family, and various knickknacks.

Buster padded in and eyed the place, his nose in the air sniffing the myriad smells that formed a picture in his mind. A cat was hiding nearby, eggs had been recently cooked, while a tingly smell of lemon-scented furniture polish reminded him of his old home. He noticed the smell of lavender in the dried flowers on the end table, and the unmistakable burst of sweat that beaded on the male homeowner's forehead. Buster went to the corner of the room, sat on his haunches, and kept a wary eye open.

Ed shut the front door and locked the interior doorknob, then flipped the deadbolt until it properly engaged with the strike plate. The sound echoed in the room. Methodically, he checked each window lock and pulled the shades together, clipping each one with a clothes pin.

"I'm sorry," Ed said as he made eye contact with Ryan. "You can't stay here."

"Hun," Helen protested, "they just got here. We made a promise to the Mannings and I intend to keep it. We can't turn them away."

"I suppose not," Ed grumbled. "You can only stay here the night then you need to get going."

"Edward Reynolds!" Helen exclaimed. "That's no way to treat these good folks." She took Ryan by the arm and coaxed him to come with her. "I'm going to make you and your friend a sandwich." Helen turned to Cassie. "Dear, what was your name?"

"Cassie."

"Cassie, will peanut butter and jelly be okay?"

"Yes, ma'am. I'd love a pb&j about now."

"Would you like sweet tea?"

Cassie nodded. "Yes. Thank you."

Helen directed them to the kitchen table, inviting them to take a seat. Ed stood in the corner, scowling, his arms crossed. His eyes kept bouncing from the kitchen window to the back door. Ryan noticed his apprehension, and the third trip he made to the door, double checking it was locked. "Is your dog hungry?" Helen asked. She washed her hands using water from a plastic jug.

"He's always hungry," Cassie said.

"Well, let me get him cat food. I don't have any dog food. He'll eat cat food won't he?"

"Sure. He'll eat anything."

Helen quickly prepared two sandwiches, sliced an apple, and poured two glasses of sweet tea. Buster crunched noisily, finishing the meal as if he hadn't eaten in days. After Ryan inhaled his sandwich, Helen asked if he'd like another one.

"If you could spare another one, yes please," Ryan said. "I'd be most appreciative."

Cassie nibbled at her sandwich, washing each bite down with a hard swallow of tea. Her stomach protested each bite and she had to concentrate on eating, unused to eating at the late hour.

"You need to eat your sandwich," Ryan said. "There's no telling when we will eat again."

Cassie nodded, then when everyone was distracted, she slipped the rest of the sandwich to Buster.

"Helen," Ed said, "do we have any coffee left over from breakfast?"

"Yes, but it's cold by now. The thermos will only keep it warm for a several hours. I'll pour you a cup if you want any."

"Seeing how we don't have any electricity anymore, coffee it is."

Ed took a seat at the table and scooted his chair in. He glanced at Ryan and Cassie, watching them in silence as they ate. He took a big swallow of coffee, set the mug back down, and crossed his arms.

"Why are you here?" Ed asked.

"We need help, Mr. Reynolds," Ryan said. He finished the last of his sandwich and handed the empty plate to Helen, thanked her, and sat back in his chair. "My parents said if I ever needed help I was to find you. Why is that? Did you know them?"

"Yes, we knew them. They used to live next door to us. They were our best friends."

An expression of comprehension appeared on Ryan's face. "That explains why I've been having this feeling I've been here before."

"Son, you lived here until you were three, then your parents left town to go live in West Texas."

"Why?"

Ed pursed his lips and shook his head. He glanced down at his lap, unable to make eye contact with Ryan. "It was a long time ago."

Helen went to the kitchen sink, fiddling with dishes in the dish rack. She nervously stacked the plates on the counter.

"Tell me what brought you here," Ed said.

Ryan took a deep breath. "Cassie and I survived a plane that went down in the southern part of Louisiana." When Ryan mentioned the number of people who perished, Helen gasped. "We waited for rescuers, but when no one came for us, we decided to walk out of there. We've walked most of the way, been shot at a couple of times, harassed—especially Cassie—and had nowhere else to go. Our food and water have run out and I promised Cassie I would get her home to Houston to her dad. I didn't think we could get very far without help."

Ed sat in silence.

"We'll be out of here first thing in the morning. Or, if you want," Ryan said, casting a glance at Helen, "we could leave now."

"No," Helen said. "You are welcome to stay here."

Ed furrowed his brow and cast an alarming glance at his wife.

"What's wrong?" Ryan asked.

Ed and Helen said nothing.

"What is it? You need to tell me." Ryan's confusion was building. His parents had always told him he could count on the Reynolds, so their reluctance was perplexing.

Ed took a swallow of cold coffee. He set the mug on the table and ran his fingers over the rim. "Have you ever heard of Cole Cassel?"

"I have," Cassie said.

"How?"

"My dad was the prosecutor on the murder case Cole was being tried for."

"Your last name is Stockdale, right?" Ed asked.

"Yes," Cassie confirmed.

Helen put a hand to her mouth.

"How do you know my last name?" Cassie asked.

Ed could only shake his head. "You two really can't stay here."

"What is going on?" Cassie asked. "And what does Cole Cassel have to do with any of this? Last I knew he was in Houston where the trial was."

"Kids," Ed said, "this is worse than I suspected. Let me explain what has been going on. Cole is from here and we've all been following the trial. I guess he must have escaped during all the chaos and uncertainty after the EMP struck—or that's what everyone is speculating. Anyway, Cole has come back and has taken over the town. From what I've heard he killed the sheriff and has commandeered the sheriff's office, and now has several deputies working for him, along with a lot of other town folk. You're either with him or against him. And those who are against him, well…" Ed glanced at Helen, "they disappear."

"How can one man take over a whole town?" Cassie asked.

"I don't know," Ed said shaking his head. "Cole is a real persuasive man, especially when two of his goons come knocking on your door and hold a gun to your head. He's now collecting what he calls 'town rent,' meaning if you live here, you pay him or *else*."

Rising from the chair, Ed went over to the kitchen counter, dug around in some papers, then returned to the table. He slapped a piece of paper on the table.

Ryan leaned in but couldn't read it in the low light. "Mrs. Reynolds, can you bring the lantern over here?" Holding the piece of paper to the light of the lantern, he read it out loud. "Wanted, Dillon Stockdale and Holly Hudson. Reward. Dead or Alive."

"What?" Cassie gasped. "Let me see that." She snatched the paper out of Ryan's hand to read for herself. "I don't understand. What is this?"

"For some reason, Cole wants both your father and Holly, and apparently they don't care if they are alive or dead. That's why you can't stay here." Ed paused. "There's more. We've already had people nosing around here asking about you, Ryan."

"Me?" Ryan was incredulous. "What does this Cole character want with *me*? And does this mean Cassie's dad is here?"

"I don't know," Ed said. "It's late, and we all need to get some sleep. You and Cassie can share the extra bedroom we have. I'd put you on the sofa, Ryan, but you'll need all the sleep you can get. Besides, the sofa isn't long enough for you. Helen, can you get them an extra blanket?"

"There's an extra one in the cedar closet. Come along, you two," Helen said. She motioned for Cassie and Ryan to follow her. "Time for bed."

Ed followed them to the extra room. "You'll need to leave before dawn, before anybody sees you. I'll get you up before then and pack you some food so you'll have something for your trip."

* * *

Fifteen minutes later and exhausted from the trip, Cassie slipped into bed next to Ryan. Buster had found a spot in the corner of the room and was already snoring.

Ryan was on his back, his arms close to his sides, trying to take up as little room as he could on the double bed. It was next to impossible with his 200 pound 6'1" frame, although he was sure he had dropped at least twenty pounds since the plane crash. His eyes were closed because he wanted to give Cassie some semblance of privacy in case she had disrobed. He hoped she hadn't. He wasn't sure he could control himself. When Cassie slipped into bed, Ryan immediately felt a pants leg brush against him.

He let out a sigh, torn because he was relieved she was still clothed, yet disappointed at the same time.

The room was painfully quiet, sans Buster's snoring, and Ryan tried to be as still as possible. Unable to sleep, he said, "Are you awake?"

"Yes."

"I can't sleep either. Want to talk?"

"About what?"

"About what's going on," Ryan said. He rolled onto his side to face Cassie. "A lot of this doesn't make sense, especially how weird Helen and Ed acted when they realized it was me. I was expecting a warm welcome, not this *you can't stay here* business."

"I can't figure it out either," Cassie said. "That wanted poster of my dad and Holly is straight out of the Old West. Do you think my dad is here?"

"I don't know. I'll ask Ed in the morning. Let's try to get some sleep. We're gonna need it."

* * *

In the next room, Ed and Helen spoke in hushed tones.

"Hun," Helen said, "don't you think you should have told Ryan the truth?"

"No, and I don't plan to."

Chapter 25

Elmer, the man who lived across the street from Ed and Helen Reynolds, had stormed out of his house, cursing at his old lady for preparing him yet another cold dinner of spam and rubbery green beans from a can.

"Good for nuthin' wench," he mumbled. He slammed the door hard, rattling it. The damn dog from next door, which barked incessantly at all hours of the day, started barking, which caused the chickens to wake and cluck. Then the rooster joined in, crowing. "Shut up!" Elmer screamed. "Shut up!"

It didn't have the desired effect because the chickens continued flapping and clucking.

Elmer stomped down the rickety steps from the back porch, kicked a toy one of his worthless kids had left, launching it across the yard and into the neighbor's yard, clipping the dog who was barking. The dog let out a yelp, tucked its tail, and slunk off to a safer place.

"Serves you right!" the man yelled.

In the darkness the dog cowered around the side of the house.

All Elmer wanted to do was to sit in his truck by himself, listen to some honkytonk music and smoke in peace, but no. The truck wouldn't start, so the best Elmer could do was to sit in silence which was what he planned to do except there were a couple of people loitering on the sidewalk at the Reynolds' house, suspiciously eyeing him over.

Standing next to his truck, Elmer patted his shirt pocket feeling for a pack of cigarettes and a light. Finding what he needed, he struck a match, lit his smoke, and took a long and satisfying drag. He immediately felt better as the nicotine took the edge off of things.

That godforsaken old couple across the street seemed to live forever, and old man Reynolds was always puttering around in his garage, straightening things, repairing broken tools, not to mention the yard work he did.

If there was a blade of grass out of place, old man Reynolds was right on it, clipping it.

Jesus Christ Almighty.

The old woman sat in her rocking chair for hours at a time crocheting and keeping an eye on the street. For a couple that didn't do anything but stay home, Elmer couldn't wrap his head around why Cole Cassel wanted him to keep an eye on them, which was when a lightbulb went off in Elmer's dim-witted brain.

Cole had paid him a visit several days prior, slipped him a hundred dollar bill, and told him more would be coming his way if he notified Colc of any unusual visitors.

"Like who?" Elmer had asked him.

"A young guy, maybe around twenty-five or so. Tall. Possibly athletic."

"Why?" Elmer had asked innocently enough.

"None of your business," Cole replied.

It wasn't so much what Cole said, it was how he said it, and Elmer had swallowed hard.

Elmer had known Cole in high school, and had heard what the guy had already done to the town since he had come back. Gossip spread fast in small-town America, since the biggest thing that ever happened was when the local funeral director had been convicted of killing his mother and stashing her body in a freezer.

That had been two decades ago.

Elmer kept an eye on the young man and woman standing on the sidewalk. When the young man asked *Can I help you?* Elmer at first wanted to ask his name and what they were doing out at this late hour. Then he thought better of it. He casually flicked his half-smoked cigarette on the driveway and stamped it out with the sole of his shoe. He slowly eased back into the shadows and when he was sure he was out of sight, he hightailed it around the side of his house, mounted the stairs on the back porch in one leap and swung open the door.

He steamrolled into the house, barreled down the hallway, and woke up his wife to tell her what was going on.

"We're gonna be rich!" Elmer said, shaking his wife on the shoulder. "Wake up."

"Huh? I told you not to drink no more." She shooed him away and put her head back on the pillow. "Go back to sleep. You're drunk."

"I'm as sober as a church lady," Elmer said. "Remember when Cole was over here last week?"

"Yeah, so?"

"He told me to keep an eye on old man Reynolds' place. He said if I saw anybody over there to let him know 'cause there'd be a big reward."

"Those people never get any visitors and they don't do nuthin'."

"I know. That's why when I saw a couple out on the lawn, I remembered what Cole told me. I've got to let him know they're here."

"It's late. Wait till in the morning," his wife said, stifling a yawn.

"No. I need to tell him now. What I need is a bike. Is there still one in the garage?"

"Yeah, but the tires are flat. You'll need to pump them up."

* * *

Fifteen minutes later Elmer was peddling to the sheriff's office as fast as his fat legs would go. He hadn't ridden a bike since he was a teenager, and the damn seat was making his butt hurt, not to mention his thighs felt like they were on fire. He was breathing hard and sweat was pouring off of his face. By the time he rode up to the office, his shirt was soaked and sticking to him as if it had been glued.

Throwing the bike down in the grass, he waddled up the sidewalk. When he came to front door, he drew a hairy arm across his forehead, mopping up sweat, trying to make himself presentable. He straightened his wet collar, hitched up his pants, and put his greasy nose to the window. He peered in.

The place was empty and dark. A desk where the receptionist usually sat was empty, some papers scattered around. A few wooden chairs were lined against the wall. File cabinets were still in place. The mayor's picture hung on the wall along with recent awards given to long-standing employees.

Elmer took a glance around. The buildings on the town square loomed dark and quiet, patrol cars sat idle, and the lack of activity gave him the creeps.

The possibility of money increased his bravado, so he gathered up his courage to check if the door was unlocked. When it creaked open, Elmer's heart pounded at a machine gun rapid pace which caused him to sweat even more.

Shit.

He was hoping it had been locked.

The place reeked of stale body odor, like there were people in here that needed a bath. He put a finger under his nose. Searching for anything to prop open the door to let some air in, Elmer found a trashcan. There, that was better.

When Elmer turned around Cole Cassel was standing behind him with a shotgun leveled at his chest.

"What do you want?" Cole asked, his voice menacing.

"Uh…uh…" Elmer stuttered. His eyes dropped to the double-barreled shotgun. "I uh…there's this uh—"

"Stop jabbering. What do you want?" Cole lowered the shotgun.

"There's uh…uh…" Elmer swallowed, took a deep breath, trying not to hyperventilate. "There's two people at the house across the street." Elmer bent over and put his hands on his thighs.

"What house?"

"The one you wanted me to keep an eye on."

"The Reynolds' place?"

Elmer nodded.

"What kind of people?" Cole asked.

"A young man and woman."

"How old?"

"I don't know. It was dark and I couldn't exactly tell."

"Think harder."

Elmer stood there like he was the third grade dunce the teacher had told to go stand in the corner.

"Okay," Cole said, "let's play a little game. I ask you questions and you answer yes or no. Can you do that?"

"Yeah."

"Good. Question one: Was the man over fifty?"

"No."

"Was the man older than twenty?"

"Yes."

"Was the man older than thirty?"

Elmer didn't answer immediately. He tried to visually remember the couple. The guy had an athletic quality about him, something about how he stood and held himself. He had a full head of hair, something Elmer hadn't had since he was about twenty. The hair was dark so he had to be fairly young.

"I think he was younger than thirty."

"Good, we're getting somewhere. Did he have dark hair?"

"Yes."

"Tall?"

"Yes."

"Courteous?"

"Yeah," Elmer said. "He asked me if he could help me. How did you guess? It's like you already know who I saw."

"You're not as dumb as people think you are," Cole said. He walked over to the front door, held it open and said, "Run on home now."

"Oh, okay," Elmer said. He stopped at the door. His mouth was dry and he licked his parched lips, unsure if he should ask for money. When he tried to talk, the stuttering started again. "Uh…I…uh…you…uh…"

"I'm a busy man, Elmer. Spit it out."

"Y-you said you'd pay me." Elmer put a hand to his mouth. He couldn't believe he said that out loud. Nobody ever questioned the boss. Ever. Elmer's shoulders shrunk down and he waited for what was sure to come. He'd seen the wrath of Cole before and it wasn't pretty.

"I did. Didn't I?"

Cole put an arm around Elmer, like they were long lost buddies then gave him a hearty slap on the back. Elmer lurched forward and eyed him suspiciously.

"I pride myself as a man of my word," Cole said, pulling out his wallet. Opening it, he took out a couple of Benjamins and handed them to Elmer.

"Thanks," Elmer said. He took the hundreds and stuffed the bills in his back pocket. "It'll help me and the missus out."

Elmer backed away as he mumbled. If Cole was going to shoot him, he'd have to look him straight in the eye. Not that it would stop Cole. By the time Elmer had exited the building and the bolt had been locked, he was only a few steps away. He stood there until Cole disappeared into the dark building.

Elmer picked up the bike, hopped on it, and started peddling away. A couple of hundreds wasn't exactly what he was hoping for, and it sure wouldn't make him rich, but it was nice what Cole had said, giving Elmer a compliment.

You're not as dumb as people think you are.

Remembering that, Elmer felt invigorated and he was overcome with a burst of pride. With that newfound sense of self, Elmer hunkered down on his bike and peddled home with gusto.

Chapter 26

"Come on, boys!" Cole barked, raking a baton over the jail cell bars. "Time to get up," he said, pacing the length of the cell. He gave the iron bars another good rake. It might as well been a locomotive in the room because the noise was deafening in the cramped space.

"Huh," Jed said, covering his ringing ears. He rubbed his bloodshot eyes, compliments from the bender of only a few hours ago. He had been sleeping soundly on one of the prisoner's bottom bunks while Cleve slept on the top bunk.

In the days following when Cole had taken over the sheriff's office, Jed had become Cole's right hand man, and if he had been a dog, he would have jumped through hoops at the promise of a biscuit. Jed wasn't the sharpest tool in the shed, but he could follow directions as long as a reward was at the end of the stick. And as long as Cole gave him step by step instructions, Jed was on it like a flea on a dog.

Decision making and critical thinking were not skills in Jed's limited repertoire, and neither was practicing at the gun range. As a deputy in the sheriff's office, he had always been told he had a better chance of being struck by lightning than drawing his service revolver. Keeping his marksmanship training up to par had slid to the end of the to-do list.

"Okay, I'm getting up," Jed growled.

"We leave in five minutes," Cole said. "You and Cleve be ready."

Jed swung his legs off the cot, and when he stood, a massive headache assaulted him. He put his hand to his head, praying he wouldn't heave right there.

What he needed was a quick remedy.

Glancing round the darkened room, he spied the whiskey bottle in the corner. He took a step forward, the room started spinning, so he grabbed hold of the bunk bed frame to steady himself. It took a second or two for the queasiness to subside. Deciding four legs were better than two, he lowered himself to the floor and crawled on his hands and knees to where the bottle was. He popped off the top and took a swig, feeling the burn of the whiskey.

He shook off the burn and after a few moments he took another swig, letting the hair of the dog soothe his throbbing headache. Soon, he was to the point he was steady enough on two feet. His bravado increased, so without wasting anymore time, Jed grabbed his pants, pulled them up, scratched his butt, then yanked the covers off of Cleve sleeping in the top bunk snoring like a freight train. He marveled that guy could sleep through a hurricane.

"Cole wants us ready in five minutes."

When there was no answer, Jed shoved him good and hard.

"Huh? What's going on?" Cleve mumbled.

"Gotta go. Now! Boss wants us."

What for?" Cleve asked. He sat up, cleared his throat, and hocked a slimy brown phlegm-filled loogie halfway across the cell. It landed with a splat.

Jed grimaced in disgust. "I don't know and didn't ask. All I know is we better be at the front ready to go in five minutes, or else." Jed let his tongue explore the soft gummy spot where a tooth used to be. He'd be damned if he was going to lose another tooth for tardiness. Jed learned really quickly Cole wasn't merciful in dishing out discipline.

* * *

Five minutes later Cole and his two henchmen were on their way. The old truck which Cole stole on his way out of Houston had been converted to the official sheriff's truck. They rigged flashing police car lights to the top of the roof and duct-taped the county logo on the side. It might have been odd, but it achieved its purpose, which was to show who was in charge.

Cole had learned a long time ago to watch his back, and tonight paranoia got the best of him, so he took a circuitous route to their destination. A dictator in power could never be too careful.

The city was as dark and quiet.

The truck rumbled down the deserted roads, headlights illuminating the empty streets with vehicles pushed to the side, waiting to be reclaimed. Flashing red and blue lights on top of the truck announced their approach.

A black cat scurried to the middle of the road and stopped, its eyes glowing yellow in the headlights. As the truck came closer, the cat bolted across the road and disappeared in a thick hedge lining a house.

Houses sat dark, their occupants sleeping. Windows were open, letting in whatever breeze came through. The peculiar scent of charcoal wafted in the still air; the smell of meat cooking tantalizing at the midnight hour.

Cole stopped the truck several houses away from the Reynolds' house. He switched off the lights and cut the engine. "Jed, all I need for you and Cleve to do is back me up. Do not under any circumstance fire your gun. In fact," Cole said, "empty the rounds in your guns and put the bullets in your pocket. Make sure there aren't any bullets in the chamber. Is that understood?"

Cleve looked shocked. "You want us to go in there unarmed?"

"Right."

"Why?"

"That's not your concern. Let me do all the shooting. You're there for backup. I don't want anyone to get hurt by accident. Got it?"

Jed and Cleve nodded their understanding.

"Good. Empty them now."

Chapter 27

"Ryan?" Cassie whispered. "Are you awake?" She nudged his arm. "Ryan?" He was snoring softly.

She woke to unfamiliar surroundings and the rapid pace of Buster's nails clicking on the hardwood floor. The mattress of the double sized bed with barely enough room to accommodate two people squeaked when she rolled over. A dark mahogany dresser circa1940s sat in the corner, a matching nightstand on one side of the bed. She reached to switch on the lamp then remembered there was no electricity.

"What'ya say?" Ryan mumbled.

"I need to let Buster out. He's been pacing, which means he needs to go out. I'm going to put him in the backyard for a few minutes."

"Okay," Ryan said sleepily. "I'll be here when you get back." Ryan rolled over onto his stomach and mashed his face into the downy pillow.

Still wearing her jeans and shirt, Cassie threw off the covers and swung her legs off the bed. "Come on, Buster. Wanna go outside?"

Buster thumped his tail, knowing what the word 'outside' meant.

Cassie opened the bedroom door, left it ajar, and tiptoed down the hallway leading to the kitchen then to the back door. Unlocking the door, she instructed Buster to go outside. Knowing it would take him a few minutes to do his business, she shut the door and went to the kitchen to get a drink of water. Out of habit, she turned the faucet to the *on* position, but only a few drops of water came out.

Hmm, right, she thought.

"Of course," she said, shaking her head. No electricity to pump water, which meant no water pressure.

Cassie checked the pantry, found a bottle of water, opened it and took a long drink.

It was dark in the house, and she let her thoughts go to her dad. Where could he be? She and Ryan had found Buster on the other side of the bridge, so her dad had to be close by, but why? What would he possibly be doing here? She racked her brain trying to think of reasons he'd be in this particular county, or maybe it had something to do with the city? Was there something she had missed? Surely he hadn't followed Cole here. She knew her parents had planned to retire to a country home, but they had always mentioned the Hill Country. The clear sandy-bottomed rivers, rolling hills and granite outcroppings, oaks that went on for miles, fertile soil, not to mention the proximity to major cities for shopping or medical care. The Hill Country definitely had all the amenities needed for country living.

After Cassie's upcoming graduation, which now was on hold, she had planned to move to wherever her parents went. While not exactly a country girl, she appreciated the lifestyle and reasons people wanted to get away from the fast pace of city life. After her mom died, her dad had lost his dream of retiring and Cassie had tried to talk him into following his dream, but his heart wasn't into it.

If only Cassie hadn't taken the flight to New Orleans, all this would not have happened. During her conversation with her dad right as the plane lost power, she told him they were descending and that they had passed the Sabine River. He had complimented her about knowing where they were, despite being at cruising altitude.

"That's it," Cassie whispered. "He was coming to find me."

Knowing how meticulous her dad was at solving problems, he must have estimated a probable location where the plane would have crashed. She put the water bottle on the counter and was bursting at the seams to tell Ryan the good news. In her excitement, she completely forgot about Buster. Coming to the bedroom door, she reached to open it—

The front door burst open!

The force of the door hit the wall and rattled it. The flimsy frame broke and wood splintered in all directions. A loose-hanging picture fell to the floor, shattering the glass into shards.

Bright beams of light blinded Cassie. She hadn't seen artificial light in a week and she put a hand in front of her face. She squinted her eyes shut at the blinding light.

A tall man wearing all black charged Cassie, and before she had time to react two other men burst in. She was immediately hit with an adrenaline dump. She turned to run, only to be jerked back when one of them grabbed her arm. The man slammed her into the wall, twisting her right arm and forcing it upwards. Her heart was beating at breakneck speed and she didn't feel the pain of her arm being twisted.

The taller of the men kicked open the bedroom door where Ryan was sleeping, flooding the room with a bright light.

Ryan scrambled out of bed and lunged for his Glock he had placed under the bed.

"Stop or I'll shoot!" the man ordered.

Lying sideways on the floor, Ryan deftly drew the Glock out of the holster, swiveled the 9 mm, and was about to sight it when the man rushed him and kicked him hard.

Ryan's hands were forced up, the gun discharged into the ceiling blowing a hole in it. A fine mist of white plaster rained down on Ryan, momentarily blinding him. He lost his grip on the Glock, yet he refused to relinquish the 9 mm.

Cassie screamed so shrilly, so viscerally frightened, it made the hair on the back of Ryan's neck stand up.

Pushing up off the floor, Ryan scrambled to his knees. It was the last thing he remembered before the brutal kick to the head.

He wobbled on rubbery legs, his brain rattling around like a shaken jar of marbles. Time and sounds slowed down to a din of garbled light and images. His eyes rolled upward, his eyelids fluttered, and he fell listlessly to the floor.

Cole Cassel knelt and rolled Ryan over on his stomach. Pulling a zip tie out of his pocket, he crossed Ryan's hands behind his back and pulled tight on the zip tie. Standing, he ordered, "Bring her in here."

Cleve and Jed forcibly shoved Cassie into the bedroom. They stood on both sides of her, holding her arms.

Her eyes zeroed in on Ryan and a worried frown wrinkled her otherwise young features. She instinctively tried to go to Ryan to help him, but was held back.

"Who are you?" Cole asked.

Cassie said nothing. She dropped her gaze to Ryan lying prone on the floor. He was still breathing, and the knowledge he was still alive provided her hope.

Cole put the spotlight on the bed positioning it so the beam shined at the ceiling. It lit up the room as if a light had been flicked on. "I'm not going to hurt you," he said.

Cassie struggled to be free of the grip the two guys had on her.

"Let her go," Cole said to Jed and Cleve.

Cassie wrenched her arms away and rubbed the sore spots where indented red marks were left. She defiantly stared at Cole.

"You his girlfriend?" Cole asked.

Cassie said nothing.

"At least tell me your name." Cole stepped closer to Cassie. "Your boyfriend is okay. He'll have a headache in the morning, but that's all. If I had meant to kill him I would have, so tell me your name."

Cassie lifted her head and stared hard at Cole, meeting his intense predator's eyes. She spoke slowly and deliberately. "My name is Cassie…" She trailed off, for some reason hesitant to say her last name. For a moment she thought she recognized the man who was standing in front of her. There was something familiar about him, and the way he spoke as if he wasn't afraid of anything or anybody. He was a man used to taking what he wanted. A shiver captured Cassie and she was jolted back to the reality that she did indeed know the man.

She swallowed hard.

"Cassie what?" Cole asked. He sat on the bed. "Cat got your tongue?"

"Cassie…" she said, taking a breath to stall, to allow her to think of a last name. If this was Cole Cassel, the man her father was about to send to the state penitentiary, there was no telling what kind of revenge he would exact on her.

"What's your last name?"

Cassie thought quickly, trying to think of a last name and as she formed the first sound of her last name, it came to her in a moment of clarity. "St-Stallman," she finally said. "Cassie Stallman."

"Now that wasn't hard, was it?" Rising from the bed, Cole reached into his front pocket and retrieved a pack of cigarettes. He struck a match on the rusted metal bed frame, lit the cigarette, and took a long drag, studying Cassie. Shaking the match out, he flicked it away.

"Do I know you?" Cole asked.

"We've never met," Cassie said with unwavering conviction. It was true.

"Hmm, for a second I could have sworn you knew me."

Ryan groaned and moved his legs.

"Okay," Cole said. "Get him up and let's go. Bring her too, and check those backpacks for weapons."

* * *

Helen and Ed Reynolds huddled together in their dark bedroom, listening to the hushed and tense voices. Knowing they were helpless against Cole and his thugs, they waited in silence for several long minutes after everyone had left and the front door had been slammed shut.

Certain the house was empty, Ed got out of bed and tiptoed to the door. He put his ear to it, listening for any sound or indication they weren't alone.

"I think they've gone," he whispered.

"Are you sure?" Helen asked.

Ed nodded.

Helen retrieved her pink bathrobe that was draped over the bed, and shrugged it on. She slid her feet into her slippers and followed her husband into the hallway. Ed ducked around the door, checking left and right, then scanned the living area of the house.

It appeared to be empty. Ed, aware of how tense his shoulders were, dropped them. "I need a drink," he said.

"Me too." Helen patted her husband on his back. "I feel sorry for Cassie and Ryan. We should have told Ryan the truth."

"What would that have accomplished?"

"He has a right to know."

"Let him learn it from someone else. The Mannings have been dead for a while, and we fulfilled the promise we made to them that we would help Ryan if he ever needed it. As far as I'm concerned, we have been released from our duty."

Feeling his way around the kitchen, Ed found a lantern and set it on the table. He turned it on, casting a cold light on the kitchen.

Helen sat down at the kitchen table and cupped her hands around her cheeks. Weariness and stress etched deeper lines on her face.

Ed took the bourbon from the top of the refrigerator and splashed a couple of ounces in a glass. He downed it in one gulp then poured a drink for Helen.

"You want a highball or have it straight?"

"Straight is fine."

With shaky hands, veined and wrinkled from age, Helen held the glass in both hands. She took a swallow, savoring the taste.

The kitchen was quiet and the old married couple sat in silence while they finished their drinks. Somewhere in the distance a dog barked, another one joined in, and when the loud and raucous bark coming from the back porch nearly burst their eardrums, they looked each other in the eyes.

Buster put his paws on the back door and popped his head above the glass-paneled door, peering in.

"The dog," Helen said. "They left their dog."

Chapter 28

"What should we do?" Helen asked.

"I don't know," Ed replied gruffly. "Bring him in, I guess."

"What do we do with him? We don't have any dog food."

"I know that," Ed said rising. He went to the back door and opened it.

Buster loped in and immediately padded to the bedroom where Cassie and Ryan had been. He nosed the bed, the floor, checking the corners, and when he realized the room was empty, he raced out with his nose to the floor. He followed the scent along the wood floor to the front door where he stopped. He nosed the floor and the splintered wood, taking in the odor of droplets of sweat left by the men.

Lifting his snout, he dismissed the myriad smells that made the house a home, and instead he focused on the one scent he recognized: Cassie's. It was different, anxious, and the hormones released painted a picture of flight or fight. She had tried both, but had been overpowered, and Buster sensed her fear of the situation.

He zeroed in on another human scent of domination, one that he had never smelled before, yet one he recognized as being powerful. He pawed at the door, whining, wanting out.

Helen pushed back from the table. "I'll let him out."

"No, let him stay here the night. I don't want a lost dog on my conscience. I've got enough to worry about." Ed polished off the last of his drink. "Let's go back to bed. I'll deal with the dog in the morning. I'm going to shut all the windows and put a dresser in front of the door. It will keep us safe tonight."

* * *

During the night Buster restlessly paced the hallways and rooms of the house like a caged animal searching for a way out. He nosed the back door, pawing at it, and when it was apparent the door had been locked tight, he raced to the front door. Buster pushed his snout to the dresser wedged up against the front door. He wiggled his body between the dresser and the front door, struggling to move the heavy mahogany dresser. The floor was slick and without being able to gain traction, the dresser refused to budge.

Backing out, he stood in the room, his canine mind whirling, trying to solve the problem. He glanced at the ceiling and back to the front door, studying the different options. He checked the back door again, then after a while, he went to the windows.

There were four windows in the front part of the house, and methodically Buster checked each one.

Using his nose, he pushed at the window pane, wiggling it, and when the pane held steadfast, he pawed the handles until he tired himself into exhaustion.

Defeated, he slunk back to the bedroom where Cassie and Ryan had slept, and with the ease of a cat he jumped on the bed. He scratched at the mattress, curled into a ball before pillowing into the side of the bed where Cassie had slept, taking comfort in her scent.

* * *

In the morning Helen opened the back door and encouraged Buster to go out. Eagerly, the large dog loped out, bounded down the stairs, and jumped over the puddle of water lining the porch.

The morning sun streamed strong and bright over the land, drying the dewy grass. Puddles of water from the recent thunderstorm rimmed the edge of the yard, while a large cistern sitting under the roof had been filled to the brim catching the runoff from the previous day's thunderstorm. Potable water it wasn't, yet it would be suitable for bathing.

"Hun," Helen called out, "I'm going to go next door to the Coopers and borrow dog food. I'll be back in a moment."

"Okay," Ed replied from the bathroom where he was shaving. "Ask Dorothy if there is anything we can do in return."

Helen rapped her knuckles on the screen door of the Coopers' house and waited for a reply. She stood there a moment, listening to the clucking of the hens and a rooster crowing. The street was quiet at this early morning hour except for the rooster. The chickens had been a real bother at first, but when Dorothy started sharing the eggs, Helen had a change of heart.

"Hi, Mrs. Reynolds," a child's voice said.

"Hi, Anna. Is your mother home?"

"Yes, but she's sleeping. She's supposed to get as much sleep as she needs. She finished taking anti…um…anti-bi-ah…"

"Antibiotics?"

"Yes, that's the word."

"Then I don't want to disturb her."

"Is there something you need?" Anna asked.

"There is. Do you have any dog food?"

"Yes. Did you get a dog?"

"Not really. We found a dog last night, and—"

"You did!" Anna exclaimed. "Can I see him? Can I play with him? Where is he? My mother said we don't need another dog after Bubbles died. Can I play with him now? Please, please."

"Slow down, honey. Yes, you can play with him. First, let's feed him. He's hungry."

"Okay," Anna said. She opened the screen door. "Don't make any noise, okay?"

"I won't," Helen whispered. "Show me where you keep the dog food."

Helen followed Anna into the kitchen where Anna retrieved a bag of dog food from the pantry. "My mom said we could feed it to the chickens if we need to. I think it's okay for you to have it."

Anna handed the bag of dog food to Helen. "Can I watch you feed the dog?"

"I guess it's alright. Do you need to tell your mother first?"

"No," Anna said, "she said not to wake her unless it's something important. Besides, she'll probably still be sleeping when I come back."

"Come on, then," Helen said.

Walking next door, Helen went to the side of the house and opened the gate to the backyard. The six foot wooden fence was too high for Buster to jump, so when Helen and Anna walked into the yard, Buster loped over to them immediately, interested in the bag of dog food.

Anna stayed behind Helen. "He's so big. Does he bite?" Anna asked. She looked apprehensively at the big, dark dog with soulful amber eyes.

"I don't think so, honey. He seems like a friendly dog. Don't get too close to him when he's eating though."

"I won't," Anna said. "What's his name?"

"I don't know. It's probably on his tags, so we'll check those after he eats."

Helen poured a large helping of the dry dog food on the ground. Buster sat patiently on his haunches, waiting until Helen had backed away before he dug into the food, his sides heaving when he took big gulps.

"Anna," Helen said, "I'm going on in. You can stay here with the dog, but don't pull on his ears or tail."

"I won't," Anna said. "I know dogs don't like that."

While Buster nosed the grass for errant bits of kibble he missed, Anna sat Indian style on the grass. She picked at a blade of grass while the dog searched for kibble, and with mounting curiosity she wondered where he could have come from. "You missed one," Anna said. She pointed to the grass indicating where the kibble was.

Buster cocked his head.

"Here," she said tapping the ground. "Right here." Anna scooted back and waited for Buster to find the kibble, but he only canted his head in curiosity. "Okay, I'll get it for you." Holding the kibble in her fingers, she put her hand out for Buster to take it. He swung his head side to side, sniffing the air. Holding the kibble in her outstretched arm, Anna inched a little closer until Buster nibbled the food out of her fingers.

"Good dog," she said. Finding another piece of kibble, Anna repeated the game for several minutes until Buster was comfortable enough for Anna to pet him. She stroked him on his head, behind his ears, and along his back. Buster sat still with his head lowered and eyes closed, letting the child pet him.

"What's your name?" Anna asked. "Is it on your collar? Will you let me check?"

Buster studied the girl, knowing that she was trying to communicate with him, indicated by her body language and rising intonation. He pricked his ears, and when she reached to his collar and jingled the tags, he didn't protest.

Anna lifted the tag and read. "Your name is Buster." She flipped the tag over and said, "If the phone ever starts working, we'll call your owner who is…" she studied the tag, "…is Dil-lon Stock-dale." Anna said the name slowly, enunciating each syllable. "Dillon Stockdale," she repeated. "What? Dillon Stockdale!" Anna stood up and her face morphed into an expression of comprehension and excitement. Without saying another word, she hurried out of the yard, slamming the gate behind her, then raced to her house.

She bounded up the front porch stairs, threw open the door and went to her mother's bedroom.

"Mommy, Mommy!" Anna cried. She gently shook her mother. "You have to wake up."

"Hmm?" Dorothy said. "What's going on?"

"Mommy, do you remember that nice man who helped me get your antibiotics when you were sick?"

"Yes."

"His dog is next door. Mrs. Reynolds said they found the dog last night and she came over to get dog food, and I was playing with him this morning watching him while he ate, and when he couldn't find all the dog food, I—"

"Slow down," Dorothy interrupted. She sat up in bed and asked Anna to start from the beginning. "So what you are saying is that Dillon Stockdale's dog is in the Reynolds' backyard?"

"Yes!"

"Stay right here and let me get dressed. I'm going over to talk to Helen."

Chapter 29

"It feels good to be home," Holly said, taking in the view of her house. The four riders had made it to her ranch. Holly dismounted her horse and gave the reins to Dillon.

Walking to the house, she spied two cats sitting on the front porch. The cats watched the group with vague curiosity, and when Holly walked up the porch steps, the cats meowed.

"Looks like we have cats now. At least they can keep the barn free of rats."

Holly swung open the front door of her ranch house, the cats skittering in after her. She walked in, breathed deeply, and took in the essence of her house. She immediately felt better surrounded by familiar items and cherished memories.

It was mid-morning, and the horses had already been put in the barn, stripped of saddles, bridles, and other equipment, and were now languidly eating hay that had been spread out for them.

Dillon wiped his boots off on the porch before he came in, then again on the mat inside the front door. Chandler followed suit, also cleaning his boots on the mud chucker.

Amanda stepped inside. She let Nipper off the leash and he nosed the new surroundings and the cats. There was the usual sofa and recliner, coffee table, magazines, books, family pictures.

Amanda's eyes flicked to the corner wood-burning fireplace stacked with firewood, seasoned and ready to be used.

"Chandler, Amanda," Holly said, "make yourself at home. This is your home now, so please, use whatever you need. There is one bathroom upstairs, and another one at the far end of this room, but don't use the toilets."

"What are we supposed to do?" Amanda asked.

"Dillon, Chandler," Holly said, "you two will need to dig a latrine for us to use. Can you make that a top priority?"

"We'll work on it tomorrow," Chandler said.

"Tomorrow I'm going back to where we last saw Buster," Dillon said. "The weather has cleared and it shouldn't take me too long to get to where he disappeared."

"I'll come with you," Chandler said. "You may need backup."

"Thanks, I appreciate that."

"Excuse me," Amanda said. She picked up a vase, letting her fingers trace the pattern. "What exactly is a latrine? Is that an outhouse or something?" Her grandfather's house still had running water thanks to a windmill driven pump, so a latrine was yet another EMP inconvenience.

"Yup," Dillon said. "Better get used to it. We'll be roughing it for a while."

Amanda grimaced at the idea of *roughing it*. She put down the vase and walked over to the covered breezeway leading from the living area to the kitchen, and stopped at the bricks cemented in a circular pattern. Plexiglass was bolted into the cement. "What's this?"

"That's a water well," Holly said. "It's a long story, but the short of it is that when my parents bought this place, they didn't want to tear down the original house. This water well was where they wanted to build an add-on so instead of bulldozing it over, they incorporated it into the house. Kinda cool isn't it?"

"Yeah, for sure." Amanda hesitantly peeked down the large cistern shape. "There's water in there?"

"Yes, and it still works," Holly confirmed. "Dillon is supposed to rig up a pulley system so that we have access to it."

"We can drink it?" Amanda asked.

"Of course," Holly said. "It will be our main source of water."

"Where do you want me to sleep?" Amanda asked.

"Upstairs there are several rooms to choose from. The one in the back is mine…" Holly hesitated and glanced at Dillon to gauge his reaction. He nodded, so Holly said, "and Dillon's. You can take either room on the other side. Chandler, you can pick out a room too."

"Okay," Amanda said. "I'm going to check it out now, and put my things up."

* * *

For the rest of the day, Dillon and Chandler went about the business of gathering firewood, checking food supplies, formulating who would hunt, and what types of supplies they could trade with neighbors. They took a quick stroll among the pecan trees by the branch, inspecting the hulls, estimating the nuts should soon be ready for harvesting in early December. The fat and calories would supplement their diet.

On a previous excursion, Dillon thought he had seen wild persimmon trees and mustang grape vines. Dewberry vines were abundant, but the fruit wouldn't be ripe until late April. An ornamental loquat tree planted in the front yard would now come in handy when the golden fruit ripened.

The garden that had been tended to by the previous caretaker still had some vegetables that the deer and rabbits hadn't eaten the tops off. Beets, carrots, cauliflower, and Brussel sprouts were root vegetables everyone would need. Potatoes and yams would have to wait to be planted until after the last spring frost.

"We'll need to repair the fence around the garden," Dillon said, walking the fence line, taking note of the holes. He pushed on a post testing the sturdiness of it. "Hey, Chandler?"

"Yeah?"

"I think a few of these posts need to be replaced, otherwise the deer will be having a smorgasbord. They'll be able to push this over in no time at all."

Working the rest of the afternoon, the steady sound of hammering could be heard as Dillon and Chandler repaired the holes in the fence and replaced posts. After that chore was finished, they added extra chicken wire at the bottom of the fence to keep out rabbits and other nocturnal animals.

Dillon was thankful for the laborious work because it didn't allow him time to think about his daughter. However, during a break in the work, Dillon mind went to his daughter and he second guessed his actions. Had there been anything he could have done differently? Maybe he should have stayed in Louisiana where he could have searched for Cassie, even if it was her remains he ultimately found.

As he and Chandler rested under the shade of a large pine, Dillon wondered if there could be any chance, even a minute one, that Cassie could be alive. He'd probably never know exactly what happened, and the decision to leave Buster behind tortured him. Holly had been right because the storm was too intense to ride it out in the open. One lightning strike could have had disastrous consequences.

Tomorrow, he'd set out at first light to find his beloved dog.

For the next hour, Dillon and Chandler pulled weeds, tilled the soil, and checked the garden for any vegetable plants that had survived the heat, resulting in late season produce.

"Hey!" Chandler exclaimed. "I found some squash and a few tomatoes."

"Great!" Dillon replied. "Gather them and let's head to the house."

* * *

While Dillon and Chandler worked outside, Holly and Amanda took inventory of the remaining food supplies in the pantry.

Holly started a list of non-perishable items like flour and pasta, sugar and salt, spices, boxed food, canned vegetables and fruit, and other sundry items such as soup and spaghetti sauce. It was a mundane, yet important task. She catalogued each item along with the quantity, then stacked each item in an orderly fashion in the pantry.

She also catalogued the remaining laundry detergent and bleach, thinking of how they could wash clothes. With any luck, there'd be a tub in the barn she could use. The bleach would be an important commodity because when toilet paper ran out, strips of sheets could be used for sanitation purposes then soaked in bleach, rinsed, and hung out to dry.

Because food would have to be rationed, Holly surmised everyone would be tightening their belt buckles soon. A life like her ancestors had from the 1800s, farmers who were lean and weathered from a life where brawn was needed. Not necessarily a bad life, only a different one.

Fortunately, Hector had kept the pantry stocked, and if an item was close to the expiration date, he had permission to use it. Although when push came to shove during hard times, an expiration date wouldn't matter. Hunger would drive a person to eat most anything.

Holly also took note of the items her mother had used in canning fruits and vegetables, such as jars, rims, and lids. For the life of her, Holly had never been interested in how the work was done. She sorely regretted not paying any attention to the methodology. Surely, hopefully, there'd be a pamphlet or cookbook somewhere in the house explaining the procedure.

Holly briefly thought about Hector and his untimely and unnecessary death at the hands of Cole Cassel. When Holly and Dillon had first returned to her house, the flock of buzzards in the nearby pasture had alerted them to the likelihood that Hector's body was probably there. There had been no time to search for a body, and Holly made a mental note to ask Dillon to search for his remains.

Amanda was sitting at the kitchen table, sipping on a warm Coke. "Holly, how long do you think this EMP thing will last?"

"Probably a long time," Holly said. "For now, we need to get through it and survive. Amanda, what do you plan to do?"

"I guess stay here a little while. Like my grandpa told you, he has a younger sister, actually about my dad's age. She has a ranch in Central Texas. Chandler said he'd take me there."

"You know you're welcome to stay here as long as you want to."

"I know, but family's different."

"I understand," Holly said. "It's getting late. Let's find something to cook for dinner tonight. I'll get a fire going outside."

"Okay, I'll help you and…" Amanda turned toward the front of the house. "What was that?"

"I think someone is knocking at the door," Holly said.

The sound came again.

"Someone *is* at the door," Holly said. "You stay here. I'll see who it is."

Chapter 30

Earlier that day, Dorothy Cooper and her daughter Anna paid a visit to their next door neighbors, Helen and Ed Reynolds. Their relationship had never been a good one because of several issues, including the discord Dorothy's chickens had caused.

Dorothy believed in a low maintenance yard, which meant letting the grass do what it wanted, and simply mow it a couple of times in the summer, while Ed's yard could have been in a home and garden magazine, so she was pleasantly surprised at his congenial attitude toward her when she paid him a visit. Ed had a box of tools and was repairing the front door.

"Ed," Dorothy said, "can you tell me where you got this dog?" She motioned to Buster who was leashed, sitting obediently next to Anna.

"The dog belongs to a friend of Ryan Manning. He's the son of our good friends, the Mannings."

"They used to live around here, right?"

"Yes. It's been over twenty years since they left."

"Why is the dog here?"

"What does it matter to you? Do you want the dog? If so, you can have him."

"No, I'm trying to figure out how the dog showed up at your house."

"Oh," Ed said. "Ryan Manning showed up here last night needing help. He was trying to get some girl back to Houston, and they needed rest and food. And because we promised his parents we would always be here for him, we let them stay the night."

Dorothy looked at Buster then at Ed. "Why did Ryan have the dog?"

"The dog belonged to his friend, Cassie Stockdale"

"Dillon Stockdale's daughter. Where are they now?"

"I don't really know how to tell you this," Ed said. He closed the front door, stepped out onto the porch, and glanced both ways. "Cole Cassel and a couple of his henchmen kicked in the front door last night, roughed up Cassie and tied up Ryan," he said in a low voice. "There was nothing we could do. You have to believe me."

"I believe you."

"They took them away. I'm guessing to the old sheriff's office on the town square."

"Why?"

"I have no idea," Ed said. "We don't want to get involved. I'm sorry. Why's this important to you?"

"Because this dog belongs to Dillon Stockdale."

"How do you know that?"

"His collar."

"Oh," Ed said. "How do you know Dillon Stockdale?"

"A couple of weeks ago he helped Anna get my antibiotics at the drugstore. He saved my life." Dorothy paused. "If Cole knows that Cassie is Dillon's daughter, he'll kill her."

"I'm not so sure he knows who she really is because when Cole pressed her for her last name she said Stallman."

"Then she must know who Cole is."

"I guess so," Ed said.

"I need to let Dillon know that Cole has his daughter."

"How are you going to do that? You don't even know where he is."

"Actually, I do know. Ed, can I borrow your bikes?"

Chapter 31

Holly cautiously went to the front door and peeked through the sheer curtain so she could get a cursory look at who had knocked. Through the opaque curtain she saw the hazy image of a woman standing back from the door, along with a child and a large dog.

The woman had big, soulful eyes. Her hair was sprinkled with gray, her skin prematurely wrinkled from the sun and the worries from living a difficult life, yet Holly believed she recognized the woman.

Holly put a hand to her face, questioning if her eyes were tricking her.

"Who is it?" Amanda asked, coming up to Holly.

"I'm not sure. I think it's…"

Holly opened the door and Buster bounded in, his excitement unbridled recognizing the house and the scent of his owner. Buster bolted through the living area, skirted around the water well in the breezeway, and ran to the back door. He jumped up and put his paws on the window, scanning the backyard, the garden, and pasture land beyond. When Buster saw Dillon in the garden, he whined and scratched at the window to be let out.

Standing on the front porch were Dorothy Cooper and her

daughter Anna.

When Holly got over the shock of seeing a classmate from thirty years ago, her eyes went to the wisp of a child standing next to her. "You must be Anna."

The child nodded.

"Dillon told me how brave you were, helping your mother get her medicine."

Putting her arm around Anna, Dorothy smiled at her daughter. "She's a great kid."

Holly was in awe of the bonding moment between mother and child, and for a brief instant she realized the tender moments she had missed out on.

"It's good to see you, Holly," Dorothy said.

"Please come in." Holly motioned for them to enter the house. "Amanda, please go get Dillon, and pour a bowl of water for Buster."

Dorothy and Anna shyly entered the house. It had been a long time since Dorothy had set foot into a house this grand. She was unsure what to do.

"Have a seat, please," Holly said. "Can I get you anything? Water, something to eat?"

"Water would be fine. Thank you," Dorothy said. While Holly was in the kitchen, Dorothy brushed off her pants before she sat down stiffly on the sofa. Unsure what to do with her hands, she folded them in her lap. Anna's gaze landed on the bookshelves and she squinted trying to read the titles.

Holly returned with two glasses of water. She handed them to Dorothy and Anna. "You can borrow a book if you want to."

Before the child could speak, Dorothy cut in and said, "We don't want to impose on you."

"It's no imposition at all. I'd be honored to lend a book to Anna," Holly said.

Anna waited for her mother's confirmation.

"Only one."

With great merriment, Anna skipped to the bookshelves and perused the titles. Buster came trotting into the room, went to Holly, and put his chin on her leg.

"Dorothy," Holly said, absentmindedly petting Buster, "I have so many questions for you. First of all, thank you for bringing Buster to us. Dillon will be so relieved that you found him. Where was he? How did you find him? It had to have been difficult to get here."

Dorothy cleared her throat. "I need to speak to Dillon."

"Of course," Holly said. "I'll see what's taking him so long. I'll be back in a—"

The front door swung open and Dillon and Chandler came in, followed by Amanda. Buster loped over to Dillon, wiggling and curling around his legs. Dillon dropped to the floor and rubbed his dog vigorously along his head and back.

"Where did you find him?" Dillon asked, letting Buster lick him all over his face.

"Dillon," Dorothy said, "I know where Cassie is."

Chapter 32

"What? What did you say?" Dillon rose from his kneeling position and looked pointedly at Dorothy.

"I came to tell you that your daughter is in town."

"My daughter?"

"Yes."

"She's *alive*?" Dillon's words were breathless. "Are you sure? I can't believe this. It's the best news I've ever had. I thought she was dead."

"Dead?" Dorothy echoed.

Dillon put hand to his forehead. "It's a long story. I knew she wasn't dead, even after everybody telling me she was. Where is she, why didn't you bring her here?"

"Dillon," Dorothy said, swallowing hard, "I don't know how to tell you this…"

"Tell me what?"

For the next several minutes Dorothy explained that Cassie and her friend Ryan, who she said was another plane crash survivor, had made their way to Hemphill. They had spent the night at her next door neighbor's house, resting and stocking up on supplies before Ryan planned to escort Cassie to Houston.

"I don't understand," Dillon said, "what were they doing at your next door neighbors'?"

"For some reason, the Reynolds owed Ryan's parents a favor, and he showed up there for help. That's all I know."

"Why were they going back to Houston?"

"Because Ryan told Cassie he would help her get home."

"She doesn't know about me being at Holly's ranch, does she?"

"I don't think so," Dorothy said.

"Of course. It makes perfect sense. She thinks I'm in Houston waiting for her."

"From what Mr. and Mrs. Reynolds told me, Cassie had no idea you were here."

"Why didn't you tell her?" Dillon asked.

"I didn't know they were next door until..."

Dillon sat down next to Dorothy. "What?"

"I'm sorry, let me finish the rest of the story. I'm not sure how to tell you this."

"What are you talking about?" Dillon asked.

"Remember how scared I was when you brought Anna home?"

Dillon nodded.

"And how I said you needed to leave because Cole has spies all around? I was right about that. Someone told Cole that you were at my house and the next day he paid me a visit. He wasn't any too nice about it. I'm sorry, Dillon, I had to tell him that you and Holly were going to Louisiana to try to find your daughter."

"So he does know I'm here. Damn. Tell me what else you know."

"I only put two and two together after I gave the Reynolds dog food and when Anna checked Buster's tags. I asked the Reynolds what they were doing with your dog and that's when they told me about Cassie and Ryan being there."

"Well, let's go get her," Dillon said. "Wait a minute. If Cassie was next door then why didn't you bring her home to me? What's wrong?"

"I'm sorry, Dillon."

"What is it?"

"Cole Cassel has Cassie."

Chapter 33

Dillon rocketed up off the sofa. "What do you mean, he has Cassie?"

"This morning Ed Reynolds told me that Cole and two of his henchmen broke into their house late last night, beat up Ryan, zip tied him, and took him and Cassie. Ed thinks they were taken to the sheriff's office near the town square because Cole has taken it over as his base of operations."

"Why did he take them?"

"I don't know. If Ed knew, he didn't say."

Dillon swiveled, facing Chandler. "I'm leaving now to get Cassie. Come with me."

Chandler, who had been leaning against a wall, took a step toward Dillon and put a hand on his arm, stopping him. "Dillon, it's getting dark, and if we go blazing into town without a plan, anything could go wrong. A sheriff's office might have a night vision equipped rifle, leaving us sitting ducks in the dark. We have to think this through if you want everyone to come home."

"I almost lost her one time," Dillon said. "I'm not going to lose her again. Don't you understand? Cole will kill Cassie because he wants to get back at me."

"Dillon, wait," Dorothy interrupted. "Cole doesn't know Cassie is your daughter. Ed said that when Cole pressed her for her last name she said Stallman."

"Oh, thank God. She must have recognized him from his pictures online. She told me she was following the trial online. Then Cole must be after her friend." Dillon hesitated. "What was his name?"

"Ryan," Dorothy said.

"Why would he want Ryan?" Dillon asked.

"Don't know."

"Even if Cole doesn't know who Cassie is, she's only safe for a little while," Dillon said. "I don't plan to lose her again.

"We're not going to lose her," Chandler said. "You're too wired up right now and too emotionally connected to think clearly. Take a deep breath and let me formulate a plan. I know the town square like the back of my hand, so let's sit down and start stacking the odds in our favor. Holly, can you get me pencil and paper?"

"Yes," Holly said.

"We'll be at the dining room table."

Holly riffled around a dresser drawer, shuffling papers until she found a legal pad and several pencils. Digging further, she found graph paper. Without bothering to close the drawer, she hurried to where the men were sitting, and handed the pad and pencils to Chandler.

"Graph paper," Chandler acknowledged, taking the pad. "This will work better."

Holly sat to one side of Chandler, while Dillon was on the other side. Amanda and Dorothy stood to the side, while Anna sat quietly in the living room reading a book.

Tearing off a piece of graph paper, Chandler used a pencil to draw the layout of the one-story sheriff's office, located cattycornered to the courthouse. He told the others he had been an unwilling resident of the jail for a few nights before the EMP struck.

Chandler carefully estimated the length of the front of the office, drawing a straight line, then indenting it where the plate glass windows were. He traced the rest of the building into a rectangle then meticulously penciled in desks and chairs, walls and doors, the break room, hallways, the bathrooms, and conference rooms. Toward the back were four holding cells.

Handing the drawing to Dillon and Holly, he instructed them to memorize the interior. "Pretend you're walking into it and having a conversation with someone. Visually imagine the rooms and where the furniture is."

"This is quite good," Dillon said.

"Like I said, I was an unwilling guest there."

Using a fresh piece of graph paper, Chandler drew where the buildings were on the town square on the street grid. He labeled the streets, and to the best of his recollection, he drew the town square.

The stores included a café, an antiques store, a few empty buildings, a home health care business, clothing, realtor, insurance agency, all of which were centered around the three-story courthouse.

"The county courthouse was built in the early 1900s with a grand staircase leading up to the second floor which houses the county clerk, district clerk, county judge, land records, oil and gas records, and just about any paperwork and records dealing with the county," Chandler recited. "The first floor, only accessible through an inside staircase, contains historical records and old furniture. The dome and clock tower were destroyed during a fire in 1909 and never replaced.

"I'm telling you all of this because I won't be positioned there."

"Why not?" Holly asked.

"For a several reasons. The roof isn't easily accessible because I'd need a ladder to climb to it. The roof also is too slick and I don't have a good line of fire from the courthouse to where Cassie and Ryan are being held. Besides, I have to be able to get down quickly in case something goes wrong."

"What about the water tower?" Dorothy suggested. "It's really high and has a panoramic view of the city."

"I'd be a sitting duck up there and wouldn't be able to get down quick enough if someone spotted me. My only choice is the Feed Store Café, which is less than a hundred yards away from the sheriff's office. It has an awning that will conceal my climb from the street, and the roof is the highest of the buildings. From a distance standpoint, the shot is easy and wind will not be a factor. The only potential problem will be the glass, but I'm almost positive it's not bulletproof. If things go to hell in a handbasket, I can run to the sheriff's office using the adjacent roofs in order to back you up."

Chandler took a breath.

"What do you want me to do?" Holly asked.

"Let me think a minute." Chandler asked for the drawing of the sheriff's office in order to check it, making sure he hadn't left out any detail, regardless how insignificant it may seem. Even the coffee pot was labeled, the pencil holder on the front desk, stapler, rulers, phones because in theory, any of those items could be used as a weapon. He rotated the paper back to Dillon, then explained the building configuration from memory.

While the plan was being discussed, Dorothy found three Styrofoam cups and poured beer into each one. Setting the cups on the table, she said, "It's warm, but it's better than nothing."

Chandler took a swallow, letting the drink take the edge off the tense situation. "It's perfect." He gulped the rest down and gave the cup to Dorothy. "Okay, Holly, you'll be the decoy. I want you to go to the front and knock on the door."

"You've *got* to be kidding."

"No. Women aren't as threatening as men, and Cole won't know what we have planned. You make him think you are alone and that you aren't armed. You make some sort of excuse regarding why you're there—"

"He's not stupid," Holly interrupted.

"Right," Chandler said, "but he is a man, and you two have a history. You're a woman, so use your womanly wiles." He put up a hand to stop any protest. "Don't give me any grief about that either. You use everything God gave you, and since you aren't as physically strong as Cole, you'll have to use your wits to outsmart him." Chandler looked at her more closely. "Didn't you two have a child together, and didn't that have to do with you representing Cole?"

"Yes," she snapped, pissed at Chandler's ability to see the truth about human nature.

"Something about he'd tell you the child's name if you won the case."

Holly nodded.

"Okay, good. Use that. And while you're distracting Cole, Dillon will be at the back door, prying it open."

"A crowbar will do the trick," Dillon said.

"Just keep it quiet, and be sure to look out for booby traps, since

Cole is supposed to be so sharp." Chandler meant it, although there was some sarcasm in his voice.

"Holly, Dillon mentioned a stash of guns under the floorboards. Could you show me, because I don't want you going in completely unarmed. Also, do you wear an underwire bra?"

"Yes, why?" She offered an offended expression as she pointed down to her parents' secret stash of guns.

Chandler rummaged through the pile and smiled, searching for a particular item. He kept the tone strictly business, resisting the temptation to make a joke. "There's an ingenious holster called a Flash Bang, which hangs a small pistol from mid-point of a bra. I can't find the holster in here, but I can rig one up. You just happen to have the perfect gun for the job. Dillon, can you get me a canvas tarp and some copper or light gardening wire?"

Dillon returned momentarily with a roll of copper wire and pliers with snips. He placed a dirty painter's tarp on the floor because he knew Holly did not want it on her good dining room table.

"This gun is a Kel-Tec P32, which features a seven round magazine plus one in the chamber. It's not much bigger than a weak .25 auto, but packs a lot more power in a lightweight package." Chandler unloaded the gun and handed it to Holly. "Try the trigger."

"Why?"

"So you'll know how it fires. It's called dry firing. It's okay, it's unloaded."

Taking the gun, Holly pointed it at a light switch and pulled the trigger. "It's pretty hard to pull, but I can do it."

"I just wanted you to note that a heavy trigger pull causes the gun to pull downward if you aren't careful. If you have to shoot, shoot two or three times to the chest, then move to the head. Some people take time to die, and you don't want to give them time to take you with them."

Holly looked toward Dillon for input.

"Listen to the man. He knows what he is talking about." Dillon held out his hand. "Hand it to me. I'll load it up for you."

Chandler passed the ammo box to Dillon. "Holly, take off your shirt. I need to see what I have to work with." Chandler immediately regretted his poor choice of words and before he could correct his statement, the heat rose in his cheeks, reddening them.

"I see why you never went into politics," Holly smirked. All of them broke into hearty laughter, and the tenseness of the situation evaporated. Even Dorothy, standing outside the room, gave a rare belly laugh.

Holly removed her shirt and draped it over a chair.

Standing close to Holly, Chandler fiddled with the copper wire Dillon had given him earlier. He created a wire connection in the middle of the bra, securing each end to the underwire. He then looped several times to create a central backing from which the main retention wire would be attached.

It was an awkward moment, seeing that Holly had her shirt off, and while Chandler worked he couldn't help but notice her assets covered in a nice lacy bra.

Sensing the awkwardness, Holly said, "Next time, I'll wear a bra equivalent to grandma panties."

Dorothy chuckled under her breath, while Dillon cracked a smile.

With the support reinforced, he made a wide wire hook to hold the trigger guard of the P32 securely in place. "I am hoping that this gets past a search. Your proportions should offer adequate camouflage," Chandler said without emotion.

"Mr. Spock couldn't have said it better," Dillon teased.

"Holly, if you have to shoot," Chandler said seriously, "don't stop until your target is dead. If you shoot at the head, shoot into the flat areas of the skull so that a shot doesn't glance off by accident. Once you have made your shots, keep your gun and also pick up your opponent's gun. Step outside immediately so I know that you're alright."

Holly nodded her understanding.

Dillon passed the now loaded P32 to Chandler, who placed it for a right handed shooter. Chandler bent the wire loop upward to secure it to Holly's bra. "All you have to do is grab the grip firmly and pull down. Don't put your finger in the triggerguard until the gun is on target. You should be able to get past a cursory 'feel up'."

"Thanks, I'll walk around and get used to it." Holly paced around the room until she showed no outward signs of her new discomfort. Cole was smart, so she could not take any chances.

"I saw a handgun that I would like to borrow, if it is okay," Chandler said, Holly nodded. He pulled a Smith & Wesson Model 29 .44 magnum revolver from the stash. "Your dad is a man after my own heart. Is it too late to be adopted?"

"Perhaps we can make an exception for you." Holly winked at Chandler.

Dillon motioned to the dusty grayish white painter's tarp Chandler had asked for earlier. "Will this work for you?"

"Perfect," Chandler said. He shook it, sending dust motes floating into the air.

Holly sneezed.

"All I need to do is to paint and texture it enough that it looks like the feed store roof from a distance."

In real life, objects, like a roof, were not perfect. There were few straight lines in nature, dirt dulled colors over time and made surfaces non-reflective, while weathering took away that new luster. Chandler knew this and shot the tarp several times with black spray paint to simulate sloppy repairs with tar. He used fireplace ash with glue to create a dirty, weathered look. Sewing a ball cap underneath the front section of the tarp would allow him to don the covering quickly and to move hands free to his firing position.

Chandler continued to sew without looking up. "Dillon, could you go over your role?"

"I'll enter the back using the crowbar while Holly enters the front of the station. Dorothy will give me the hand signal to go in. Next, I'll move through storage and into the cell area, watching for any booby traps," Dillon recited. "I'll neutralize Cole's two henchmen if they are in the area, free the hostages by whatever means necessary, and move them back out the door. Once we are out safely, Dorothy will fire three shots as a success signal and Holly will exit the front door while Cole investigates the shots. Chandler, you will take out any unfriendly party that follows Holly out the front door. Did I leave anything out?"

"That's the plan in a nutshell," Chandler said. "If something goes wrong and Holly does not reappear, I'll leave my position and rush for the front door using handguns. If the operation lasts more than seven minutes, I'll retrieve Holly by force and we'll try to determine what happened to you and the kids."

Chandler looked directly into Dillon's eyes, confirming that Dillon understood he would probably already be dead if the seven minute scenario occurred.

Chandler instructed Holly to wear a loose, random patterned

shirt, one which wouldn't print a gun. She assured him she had such a shirt and went to find it.

Next on the agenda was what Dillon had to do. "With any luck," Chandler said, "they'll come out to the front room to see what's going on with Holly, leaving only one person in the back."

Since the county jail was ancient, Dillon would need to find a key to the cells. "I can pick the lock if necessary," Dillon said. "We were taught that in the military, and fortunately I packed my lock-picking kit in my original bug-out bag I brought here. I know old locks tend to be stiff from years of dust and excess paint."

Holly arrived with her new shirt, buttoning it. "You're a man of many talents."

Dillon winked at her. Holly tossed him a knowing smile.

"Okay," Chandler said, "Dillon, once you get Cassie and Ryan out of their cells, tell them to go back the way you came and hightail it into the tree cover. Take two extra pistols and give one to each of them. Be sure to warn them about Dorothy giving the all clear shots. By the way, can Cassie shoot?"

"When she needs to."

"Good enough. From there, they need to cross Market Street and head over near the post office where our horses will be. Since we're taking all three, Cassie and Ryan can double up and ride one of the horses. Give them directions to Holly's ranch.

"Holly, you'll need to position Cole near the plate glass windows where I can get a good shot. Be aware of the direction that I'm shooting from so that in case for some godforsaken reason the bullet exits Cole, you won't get the leftovers. A bullet that passes through a body can still be deadly." Chandler took a breath, then asked, "Everybody understands what they need to do?"

A quiet and tentative voice asked, "What do you want me and Anna to do?" It was Amanda.

"Sorry, I forgot about you ladies," Chandler said. "You and Anna need to stay here and guard the place. Buster and Nipper too. If anyone shows up uninvited, slip out the side window and fire warning shots when we return so that we don't ride into an ambush. And Holly," Chandler placed his focus back on her, "remember, once you get Cole into position, I'll own him. He'll never be any more trouble to you or anyone, ever."

Later that night after Dorothy, Anna, and Amanda went to sleep,

Dillon, Holly, and Chandler went over the logistics and tactics one more time until finally Chandler was satisfied.

"There's only one thing that we haven't planned for," Dillon said.

"What's that?"

"Without clocks working, how do we know what time to leave?"

"I'll take care of that," Chandler said. "I've got a built-in alarm clock. We'll need to leave no later than 5 a.m. because we need to get into position before sunrise. I estimate it will take us thirty minutes to get into town walking the horses at a moderate pace. Holly, you can come with us to the post office where we'll leave the horses, but you'll need to backtrack then take a direct route to the sheriff's office, just like you were riding there straight from your home."

"I'll do that," Holly said. "It sounds like a thorough plan."

"I think we're ready," Dillon chimed in.

"There's an old saying that no plan survives first contact. That means that some detail of the plan is bound to go wrong. You need to remember where each of us are and know that we'll do whatever we can to get everyone home. Now let's all try to get some shut-eye while we can. We're going to need it."

* * *

The night was long and sleep eluded Dillon. He tossed and turned, going over every thinkable contingency. He mentally reviewed the layout of the sheriff's office, where the furniture was, the offices, closets, file cabinets, cells, even the bathroom stalls in case someone hid in there. The wind moaned around the house, the night was dark, and Dillon finally drifted off to sleep for what seemed like a minute.

He awakened to Chandler nudging him.

"Time to go!"

Chapter 34

As Chandler had planned, they arrived at the post office about thirty minutes before sunrise. Dillon and Chandler tied their horses to the bike rack at the post office, while Holly held her horse back. Dorothy began working her way around the buildings to her position as rear lookout.

"You remember the route we talked about, right?" Chandler asked.

"Yes," Holly said.

"When you pass by the tree cover where Dillon will be hiding, you'll have five minutes to get Cole to open the door. I'll already be in position on the café."

Dillon sensed Holly's apprehension. She had been quiet during the ride from the ranch to the city, and her brow was uncharacteristically furrowed.

"You'll be okay," Dillon said in his best reassuring voice. "Stick to the plan."

Holly nodded. She pulled on the reins, spurred her horse, and disappeared in the low light. She backtracked a few blocks, turned on Highway 87, then went one block past Main Street.

The air was still and thick with dew on this October morning, and as Holly rode past where Dillon should be, she slowed her horse and using the sign they'd agreed upon, dipped her chin in Dillon's direction.

The sheriff's office came into view and the sight of it caused Holly's heart to beat faster. Cassie's life was in danger and she knew how broken Dillon had been thinking his daughter had died in the plane crash.

It was now or never.

Holly dismounted her horse, walked it over to the grass in front of the sheriff's office, and loosely tied the reins to a lamppost. She took a deep breath and went to the front door.

The door along with four panes of glass on each side was set in about four feet from the building façade. A large Coca-Cola vending machine obscured the view of one of the plate glass windows.

The door was locked as they had suspected. Holly knocked on the door, rattling the windows. It was dark inside and the glare of the rising sun reflected on the plate glass windows.

Holly stood there a moment, unsure how to proceed. She took a step away from the door and looked left and right. There was no movement on the street.

She just about jumped out of her skin when the door popped open and she saw Cole. They locked eyes, two people harboring ill will toward one another; one a predator, the other who could possibly become one under the right circumstances.

"Fancy seeing you here," Cole said, the first to speak. "Didn't expect to ever see you again."

"We had a deal, remember?"

"Yeah, I remember."

"You said if I won the case, you'd tell me the name of our child. I'm here to collect payment."

"You alone?" Cole asked, immediately suspicious of Holly coming here by herself.

"Yes."

"Dillon's with you, isn't he."

"He's not, Cole. I'm here by myself."

"I know he's at your ranch."

"That he is, but he's not here with me now. You know he'd never let me see you alone."

"Got a point there. Get in here."

* * *

Chandler had used an awning to fling himself onto the first roof. Now covered by his roof-colored tarp, he moved silently up to the best point needed for his sniping position. Cranking his scope up to its highest magnification, he determined the thickness of the glass by observing the window frame. About a half an inch, which meant it was not bulletproof glass, as he had suspected.

This might just work.

Chandler silently deployed his spring loaded Grip-pod on his LaRue OBR. He had already decided to use Hornady .308 165 grain Interbond Tactical Application Police (TAP) ammunition for this shot in order to maximize the chance of an effective shot through glass. The rifle was supported in the rear by Chandler's hand-adjusted bean bag, so only a precise trigger squeeze would be required. Due to the close proximity of the shot, he reduced the magnification to 4X so he could easily track any additional targets that might rush into his field of fire.

* * *

Cole opened the door and motioned for Holly to enter. Once she was inside, he grabbed her and pushed her up against the wall, hard.

She gasped.

Cole thrust a knee between her legs, making her spread them, and while she was pinned against the wall, he ran his hands along her legs, feeling for any weapons. His hands went to her waist and sides, under her arms, and when he put his hands under her bra, she slapped them away.

"I'm not letting you feel me up." Her tone was icy.

"If I wanted to, I would have," Cole replied in an equally icy tone.

Holly let out a breath she had been holding, relieved that Cole hadn't challenged her.

He stepped away. "What do you want?"

"I want to know the name of our child."

"Last I recall, you didn't win the case, and since that was part of the deal, well, you didn't deliver."

"Last I recall, you're not in jail."

"Splitting hairs at this point," Cole countered. "In case you haven't noticed I *am* in jail. The difference is I say who gets locked up and who doesn't."

Holly was innately aware that Cole was standing in a direct line to the café where Chandler was located. If he took a shot now, she'd never know the name of their child. What she did next even shocked her. Holly stepped in front of Cole, positioning herself so Chandler didn't have a good shot.

"Cole, this isn't a neighborly visit. Just tell me and—"

A strange noise came from the rear of the building.

"What was that?" Cole asked.

"Cole!" Holly said. Taking a grave chance, she slapped his face. She had to divert him, knowing it was Dillon who had made the noise.

Cole grabbed her arm and squeezed tight. "Don't ever do that again."

"Tell me. I want to know."

He squeezed harder. Through clenched teeth he said in a low voice, "Quiet."

* * *

Dorothy had waited as long as she could for Holly to get Cole's attention and had given Dillon the signal to proceed. After a quick sight and sound check of the area, Dillon sprinted out of the tree cover and to the back door. Using a towel over the crowbar to muffle the noise, he pried open the door with a deft heave.

A loose metal plate popped off and clanged to the floor, making a noise not normal for a quiet morning. He hadn't counted on that contingency.

Dillon froze. He set the crowbar on the ground just outside the door. If anyone had heard the sound, they'd be listening for it again.

Carefully, he opened the door further, slid in, and eased the door back into place. He drew his Glock and held it with both hands, pushing his shoulders forward, using the isosceles stance for better recoil control and the ability to shoot on the move.

The interior was dark. Some light shone in through horizontal rectangles of old style glass bricks dating from the 1950s or earlier. The walls were painted a dull off-white. Decades old pictures of twentieth century city living decorated the walls, along with portraits of once important city officials.

Sliding his feet inch by agonizing inch, Dillon's eyes swept over the dark interior. He listened intently for any sign of a hostile.

To his right was an empty office. Another ten feet there was a hallway running perpendicular to where he stood.

He crept forward.

Advancing to the end of one hallway, he jutted his head around the corner, getting a glimpse of the room. Inadequate light from the other end of the hallway supplied a meager amount of illumination. Several cells lined each side of the hallway. Beyond that there was a heavy door with a small window. He repeated the action on the other side of the hallway, which appeared to have a couple of broom closets.

Scanning the darkened hallway, he saw someone in one of the cells frantically wiggling in place. The woman was standing and seemed to be anchored against the bars. Dillon immediately recognized the slender form with long brown hair, because how could a father not know his own child?

Cassie, he mouthed. He was overwhelmed with the urge to run to her, open the cell, and whisk her to safety.

Common sense prevailed.

Dillon squinted to see what held her and noted zip ties on her ankles, wrists, and mouth. Putting zip ties on Cassie's mouth indicated Cole was a depraved psychopath capable of unimaginable brutality.

A taller person, a young man Dillon surmised was Ryan, was also zip tied like Cassie. Ryan shot a confused look at Dillon then looked at Cassie. She tried to say something to Ryan that Dillon couldn't understand, but whatever it was, it did not calm either of them down. They both continued to struggle against their restraints.

Dillon quietly eased to the cells holding Cassie and Ryan. He remembered what Chandler had said about traps, and proceeded with deliberate caution.

The muffled voices from the two kids intensified to the point that Dillon almost shushed them out loud. Cassie kept shaking her head and trying to say something, the meaning lost to the dire situation.

With his heart pounding, Dillon shuffled forward.

Something tugged at his cuffs, and he stopped.

A tripwire.

He placed one foot over the trip wire and had just lifted the second foot when he was hit in the back by a tremendous force, slamming him into the floor.

He instinctively put out both hands to break his fall. In the second it took to realize what had happened, searing pain gripped his hands, especially his left one. Both knees had buckled at the forceful impact.

Dillon was on the floor in push up position, and in incredible pain. He could not see his predicament, and resisted his impulse to scream out loud.

A voice pierced the silence.

"Hello, Dumbass! I'm Cleve." A figure emerged from the darkened corner. Turning up the wick on an old kerosene lantern, he asked, "How do you like our version of Twister?"

Dillon surveyed damage to his body and what had caused it.

Shit.

He had fallen for a sophisticated trap. The tripwire wasn't the trigger after all. It had been to distract him.

Dillon now understood that Cassie and Ryan had been trying to warn him of the trap. If only he had listened.

He quickly assessed his situation. He had been impaled by nails, and his left hand had three nails sticking upward through it. The Glock in his right hand had taken most of the force, although one nail was deeply buried into his thumb muscle. He was not bleeding badly, so no major blood vessels were hit.

He could still shoot, if he could free his right hand and loosen the Glock from the nails that had penetrated the plastic frame.

Cleve approached Dillon and stepped on his butt like someone would step on a stone to cross a stream. Dillon stiffened his body to keep his pelvis from being impaled by more nails. Standing to the right of Dillon, Cleve used his knife to cut down two seven gallon water jugs that were hanging on ropes. He made a point to hold one of the heavy jugs where Dillon could see it.

"I was looking for a way to disarm you without killing you. Looks like I *nailed* it!" Cleve doubled over and laughed at his own joke. "Cole is going to be so happy. By now, you're probably asking yourself how you ended up on the floor. Well, it's not smart to underestimate country boys like Cole and me. We knew you'd find the tripwire, so I just waited until you were in position and pulled the release on those water jugs. There was no way you could stay on your feet after getting hit by over a hundred pounds swinging down on your back." Cleve dropped the jug and used Dillon's butt as a stepping stone once again to get back on Dillon's left side.

Dillon was furious with himself, but knew there was no way he would have spotted that trap. He had failed his part of the rescue, and Holly could be dealing with two murderous men by herself in the next room.

"Dad!" Cassie cried in muffled frustration through her zip tied mouth.

"I spent all day hammering nails through plywood," Cleve said. "Cole said to call him after I softened you up. So I'm gonna have me some fun. Let's see you stay off the nails after this!" Cleve tensed his muscles, brought his right leg up, preparing to bring all his weight down onto Dillon.

Dillon took advantage of his only chance. He remembered from his childhood karate training how easy it was to dislocate a knee from the side.

Just as Cleve thrust his foot down, Dillon pivoted and drove his left foot sideways into Cleve's left knee, which was currently supporting all of Cleve's weight.

Cleve was caught totally by surprise and the force of the hit caused him to buckle. He fell clumsily onto the nail bed and was pierced head to toe. Laying there, impaled, he contorted his face to release a guttural scream.

Dillon could not let that happen.

He swung his lower body over on top of Cleve's, causing Cleve to sink deeper onto the nails. A nail pierced Cleve's jugular vein, releasing a copious amount of blood.

Cleve's eyes fluttered, he took a deep breath, then sank further into the nails, his life fading.

Looking at his impaled hands, Dillon steeled himself for what he had to do. Using Cleve as a pad, Dillon gritted his teeth and leveraged the weight of his lower body against the nail impaling his right hand. One quick tug and he freed his hand. He flexed it, testing if it was still usable.

"Ryan, can you shoot this?" Dillon asked, referring to the Glock that had protected his fall.

"Yes." The word was muffled.

"As soon as I free your hands, reach over and take it. You may have to shoot right away if someone comes through the door, so be ready."

Still partially impaled and unable to move freely, and with the element of surprise gone, Dillon estimated the probability of a successful shot to free Ryan. Taking the Glock in his wounded hand, he brought it up and aimed carefully at the square tab of the zip tie binding Ryan's hands. An easy shot under normal conditions, but his punctured thumb muscle had dealt him an additional helping of agony.

Dillon breathed out and took the shot.

The shot tore through the square tab, the zip tie fell loose, and the bullet lodged somewhere in the ceiling tiles.

Ryan was free.

Dillon passed the gun to Ryan.

Ryan took the gun and checked the magazine to confirm how much ammo was remaining. Dillon also passed him a pocket knife, so Ryan completed freeing himself while simultaneously watching the door. He held the semi-auto at the ready like he knew what he was doing.

Tears of frustration streamed down Cassie's cheeks. Her worry for her dad could hardly be contained.

Dillon took the knife back from Ryan and asked Cassie to lean as far over as she could so he could cut the zip ties.

"Cassie, give me a moment. We'll be alright," Dillon whispered.

Dillon sat back and panted heavily, taking a moment to gather his wits.

With one hand still impaled, Dillon braced himself for what might be the worst pain in his life. Using the power of his legs supported by Cleve's body, he grasped the fingers of his left hand with his freed right hand and pulled up with everything he had. Cradling his throbbing left hand, Dillon was assaulted by a huge wave of nausea and lightheadedness, somehow managing not to faint.

"Dad, are you okay?" Cassie asked. "Can I help you?"

"Just give me a moment."

"How did you find us?"

Dillon held up his hand. "We'll talk later. Where are the keys to the cells?"

"They're on Cleve's belt, just below his belly."

Cassie winced at the sucking sound Cleve's body made when Dillon pulled him off the nails to get at the keys.

Grabbing the keys, Dillon tossed them to Cassie. She unlocked the cell and emerged. Heading towards Ryan's cell, she stopped at the sound of a thud.

The door from the front office swung open, and Holly was violently pushed inward, being held by her hair from behind. She had obviously been beaten, with one eye starting to swell shut and her split lip dripping blood.

Dillon had placed the two pistols to be given to Cassie and Ryan in the small of his back, secured by his tightened belt. His still functional right hand moved toward a pistol.

"Stop moving or she's dead. I know you've got a pistol so throw it down on the floor in front of me." Cole shoved the deadly end of a pistol against Holly's temple. He held her by her hair just above the scalp.

Dillon glanced at Holly. She shook her head in worried consternation with a movement so minor only Dillon noticed it.

"I won't ask again," Cole said.

Dillon complied by reaching behind his back and pulling out the pistol that was on his left side. With some luck, he might get a chance to pull the remaining pistol if Cole was distracted. He tossed the pistol to the ground.

"Ryan," Cole said, "you don't want me coming in there finding any weapons."

Ryan stood up in defiance. "How do you know my name and what do you want with us? I don't even know you."

"But *I* know *you*."

"What are you talking about?" Ryan was perplexed.

Cole jerked Holly's head back. "Why don't you introduce Ryan to his real family?" Releasing her, Cole pushed her head forward hard.

Holly stumbled.

"Tell him, Holly. Tell him about our deal," Cole said, "the one about taking me as your client."

Holly swallowed. "He said that if I won the case he'd tell me who our son…" Holly glanced sharply at Ryan, and a brief moment of clarity came to her. The morning light filtered in through the window from the adjourning room, and as she looked at Ryan, she recognized for the first time a resemblance between Cole and Ryan. Those same piercing eyes, the high cheekbones, the way their hair fell over their foreheads. The same broad athletic shoulders and long legs a runner would have. In a slow and deliberate voice she said, "He said he'd tell me who our son was if I won the case."

"What? What are you talking about? What does that have to do with anything!" Ryan asked.

"I was hoping that my son wouldn't be so dense. Do I need to spell it out for you?" Cole took the tone of a disappointed teacher. "Son, I rescued you. After I found out that you were at the Reynolds', I came to get you. You're my flesh and blood. We can own this city, any city. It's a new world now, and it's ours for the taking. The only person who could stop me was Dillon, and once I learned he was here with Holly, well, the rest was easy. I knew Holly would come looking for me, and Dillon wouldn't be far behind."

"Have you lost your mind? You beat us up and kidnapped us! No father of mine would do that," Ryan said.

"Would you have come with me willingly?"

Ryan only looked at him.

"Let me spell it out for you, son. Holly's your mother and I'm your father."

"I don't believe you."

"Why else would I single you out?" Cole's face turned angry.

"I thought it was because of Cassie." As soon as the words escaped his mouth, Ryan realized what he had said.

Cole glanced at Dillon then at Cassie. "Cassie Stallman, huh? More like Cassie Stockdale." Cole laughed. "I see the resemblance now."

"Let them go," Dillon said. "It's me you want, not them."

"Actually, it's Ryan I want. You other three, not so much. Although it wouldn't be neighborly of me to kill Ryan's mother, now would it?" Cole looked at Ryan. "Son, I want you to know I've kept up with you all your life. I know when your birthday is, I know you were going to med school at Tulane, and I know it was only a matter of time before you came back here. The Reynolds are such nice people aren't they?" Cole said mockingly.

"I don't care who you say you are," Ryan said defiantly, "you're an asshole."

Cole opened his mouth to say something when the silence was pierced by four quick pops.

While Cole's attention was on Ryan, Holly had pulled the P32 from her bra holster and fired off four shots in quick succession. She did as Chandler had told her to: aim for the chest then for the head. She was momentarily perplexed at the ineffectiveness of the shots. Cole should have gone down, or at least been stunned.

During a split-second lull in the shooting, Cole took a quick step forward and slapped the P32 to the floor before Holly could adjust her aim upward. He kicked her in the stomach hard enough to knock her against the opposite wall, where she slid to the floor.

Cole ripped open his loosely buttoned shirt to reveal soft body armor with a chest-sized hard plate in the middle. Holly's shots all hit the plate, so the blunt trauma was minimized. "You three are dead now for sure!" Cole smiled like the demon he was.

Chapter 35

Sitting on the café roof, Chandler became concerned. Seven minutes, no shots from Dorothy, no targets for him, a muffled pop, then four obvious gunshots. Had his plan really gone that bad?

Action was required.

Chandler popped the rear pin of his carbine and broke it open like a shotgun. He removed the bolt carrier group and pocketed it.

He shut the OBR, pressed the rear pin back in place, and shut the dust cover, concealing the absence of the bolt carrier group which made the carbine inoperable. He left the OBR on its grip-pod under the sniper cape.

Breaking into a jog, he jumped to the next lower roof, swung himself over the last rail, and slid down to the street. He drew his Glock 17 and using an isosceles stance he headed to the front entrance of the jail.

"Throw down your gun or you're dead." Chandler stopped in mid-stride. He held his gun pointed down as he slowly turned toward the voice. The morning sun that was his friend a few moments ago now made it difficult for him to see his elevated target. What he could see was not good. Jed was in a kneeling position with the semi-automatic OBR Chandler had left on the roof.

"Drop it," Jed ordered.

Chandler tossed the Glock 17 to the pavement.

Jed stood up, still pointing the OBR directly at Chandler. "Looks like you're going to die by your own rifle. Or should I say, my new rifle." Jed laughed at his own cleverness.

Chandler smiled, but without mirth. "It looks like one of us is in for a big surprise."

Jed pulled the trigger, but the OBR did not fire. He dropped the rifle and frantically swung his slung AK around to the front.

Chandler pulled open his shirt to reveal a shoulder holster containing the 8 3/8 inch Smith & Wesson Model 29 he had borrowed from the floorboard collection at Holly's house. A fifty yard shot would be difficult for some, but not for him, and especially not for this revolver.

Jed's eyes bounced from Chandler to his AK. His hand started to sweep the safety down.

Working quickly, Chandler cocked the hammer for single action and let a 240 grain pill loose.

The impact of Chandler shot's hit Jed square on the chest.

Jed's grip on the AK loosened and it slipped downward toward the roof. He swayed, trying to take a breath, but all he got was a mouthful of blood. His eyes fluttered and he looked like a man out of breath, except for the maroon stain on his shirt just above his heart.

Chandler's dad had taught him that even a dead rattlesnake can still bite, so Chandler took solid aim and pulled the trigger double action. The second shot rang out and Jed's head jerked back. There was no doubt of a solid hit, even in the bright sunlight.

All surprise was now gone.

Chandler quickly reloaded the .44 Magnum and checked that the Glock 17 was still in good order. He entered the sheriff's office and slowly crept forward.

* * *

Hearing the muffled gunshots, Cole smirked. "Two shots. Well I guess Jed has done his job, which means the cavalry isn't coming." Cole picked up Dillon's pistol and pointed it at Cassie. His other gun was alternately pointing at Holly, then Dillon, then back to Holly.

Cole's amusement was obvious. "Who wants to go fir—"

A shot rang out and Cole stumbled backwards, stunned by the blow. His breathing became difficult and a red stain appeared on the lower part of his neck, just above the area covered by the vest. Holly and Dillon hadn't moved, and when Cole figured it out that Ryan had shot him, he pointed both guns at Ryan.

Holly screamed.

Dillon pulled his remaining pistol with his injured right hand and jerked the trigger the moment the sights landed on target.

Cole's cheekbone exploded, and he stumbled, reflexively pulling the triggers on both guns, firing wildly into the ceiling.

Dillon used the moment to place the second shot where it needed to go.

Cole slumped to the floor, a gaping hole appearing between his eyes. He took a hard breath, his body stiffened once, then he exhaled his last breath.

The door from the office swung open.

Dillon swiveled his gun in the direction.

"Did I miss the party?" Chandler asked, careful not to stick his head through the open door. His sense of humor and timing left something to be desired.

Everyone held their fire.

Dillon took a quick sweep of the room. "Is everyone alright?" He didn't hear the mumbled words of *we're okay*, *I think so*, or *I am*. All he could think of was to go to Cassie. He put his hands on her shoulders, looked at her lovingly, then pulled her close and wrapped his arms around her.

"I told you I'd come for you if anything happened," he said. "You're safe now. We're all safe."

Epilogue

In the days after the shooting, Holly explained as much as she knew about Cole and the reasons why he had become such a cold-blooded killer.

"You're nothing like him," she repeatedly emphasized to Ryan. "If Cole hadn't witnessed his mother dying and finding his father with his head blown off, I'm sure things would have been different. *He* used to be different; he used to be kind and thoughtful. He would give the shirt off of his back to you if you needed it. The Cole I knew, the one who fathered you, was a lot like you are now, Ryan. Don't let this other Cole affect you or destroy you. You can't."

* * *

With the help of some of the store owners on the town square, Cole and the two deputies were buried in unmarked graves in the wooded area behind the sheriff's office.

Holly invited Cassie and Ryan to group at her ranch house until they got on their feet and recovered from the ordeal.

Dillon drove Dorothy and her daughter Anna back to their house, using Cole's stolen truck.

Physically, the scars and scrapes disappeared, and Cassie and Ryan put back on weight they had lost.

Psychologically, it was a different story, and Ryan struggled with the newfound knowledge that Cole was his father. But as Dillon had once told Holly, there were equal sets of genes, and the good genes would override the bad ones. Holly told Ryan to hold on to that knowledge.

For a while, the tight-knit group shared in rebuilding Holly's ranch, getting the garden in shape, canning what vegetables they could find, hunting, and preparing for the winter.

Chandler and Amanda had become close and would seek quiet moments among the busy days.

Ryan and Cassie were never far apart, having bonded over their harrowing brush with death from the airplane crash, subsequent trek through the swamp, and Cole's imprisonment.

* * *

One day when the sun was low in the sky and the treetops swayed in the wind, Cassie spoke to her dad.

"I need to go back."

"Go back where?" Dillon asked.

"Home, to Houston."

"Cassie, your home is here with us, and Ryan can stay as long as he wants to. You know that."

"You don't understand," Cassie said, "I *have* to go back."

"Why?" Dillon asked.

"I need something of Mom's, something that I can hold on to, that's part of her. It would be proof that she lived. I need to hold it in my hands, something tangible she would have wanted me to have."

"It would be suicide to go back into the city now. Gangs will have formed, turf wars have probably broken out, grocery stores will be empty. People are laying dead in the streets."

"Dad, you can't talk me out of going back. I have to have something of hers."

"Cassie," Holly said, walking up to her, "I have something of your mother's." She reached behind her neck, fiddled with something, then lifted a gold chain holding an opal. "I forgot I had it on until now."

"It was my mother's favorite," Cassie said. "Where…how?" Cassie's eyes brimmed with tears.

"When I was at your parents' house that first night," Holly said, glancing at Dillon, "I was looking in your mom's closet for something to wear. I didn't mean to snoop or pry, but there was a wooden box that I was drawn to. I opened it and found this necklace. It was so beautiful I couldn't resist putting it on. I didn't mean any disrespect by it. I want you to know that. I never intended to keep it."

Cassie nodded.

"Take it," Holly said. "Your mother would have wanted you to have it. I only borrowed it for a little while, for safekeeping, for when it was needed. I know now why I was drawn to it. You were meant to have it."

"Thank you," Cassie said. A lump formed in her throat and hot tears flowed down her cheeks. She put on the necklace, swallowed once, and swiped under both eyes, blinking fast. She looked in the mirror.

Dillon was dumbstruck at how much she resembled her mother. The same heart-shaped face, round eyes, even similar eyebrows. But she wasn't her mother, she was her own person, with her own dreams and hopes for the future.

Dillon's life was here, right now, with Holly. They would build a life together and face their own trials and tribulations, living as their forefathers had done, working the land, being a family—it was what life was about.

* * *

The day came for Dillon to say goodbye to Chandler and Amanda. It was a clear day, the sky a crystalline blue with wispy clouds laying low on the horizon. There was a chill in the air and golden leaves fell upon the ground.

The pair was well fortified with food to last them a week, camping equipment, and extra ammo. Amanda had insisted on taking Nipper, having made a special carrier which was attached to the saddle.

Earlier, everyone had said their goodbyes and there had been tears and hugs, so it was Dillon alone who bid them safe travels.

Chandler and Amanda rode double on Cowboy, and while it pained Dillon to give the reins to someone else, Chandler had promised to return Cowboy one day.

Amanda was ready to rejoin her family in Central Texas, and since Chandler had promised Amanda he would escort her to her great aunt's ranch, Dillon bid them Godspeed on their trip.

It was bittersweet seeing them leave. Chandler had become Dillon's right hand man, helping him with everything from repairing fences to the more mundane work of pulling weeds in the garden.

The town of Hemphill was slowly returning to normal, yet it would be a new normal with new ways.

The county hospital was now open a few hours a day to treat minor injuries, but with only a couple of doctors and nurses, the wait time could be a day or two. A local doctor had treated Dillon's injuries, given him a tetanus shot, and told him how lucky he was to have full use of his hands.

Some of the neighboring ranch owners formed a cooperative, trading goods and services.

There had been scant news on what had caused the EMP, although some ham radio operators were picking up Russian chatter leading to speculation it was the Russians who detonated the EMP bomb. There had also been rumors of foreign troops infiltrating the bigger cities where whole neighborhoods had been destroyed, burned to the ground, entire families wiped out.

Dillon looked skyward across the treetops tinged with the glow of the morning sun. His family had survived by sheer will and fierce determination. They were together and that was what counted.

Chandler and Amanda would forge their way into the unknown, and Dillon wondered if he would ever see them again. Although Chandler had promised to return Cowboy, some promises were made to keep, some only for a while, a reality which Dillon reluctantly accepted.

Cowboy seemed to sense the change too, because when Chandler said the magic phrase, Cowboy hesitated. It took some coaxing to get the horse walking, but when he finally did, he snorted, shook his head, and proudly walked on.

Dillon waited on the road until Chandler and Amanda disappeared beyond the tree line, then headed back to the house where a woman waited with open arms, and where his daughter was with her own companion, one who Dillon hoped would be her husband one day.

Together they would forge ahead and build a new life, here, right now in this new place.

He had his family, and that was all that mattered.

He walked into the house where Buster waited.

"Come on, boy. We've got work to do."

The End

The Hunted

The East Texas woods were too silent, unnerving Dillon on this gray and cold December evening. He sat perfectly still on a canvas stool, hidden in a dense thicket of young saplings dripping with vines. He had the muzzle of his .30-06 deer rifle pointing down, ready to lift it at a moment's notice if the prized buck passed through his line of vision. There was something inherently satisfying about going on a hunt to put meat on the table. The problem was he didn't realize *he* was the one being hunted.

An hour earlier, Dillon was getting ready. Cassie and Ryan had gone to a neighbor's house to trade goods.

Sitting on a kitchen chair at the ranch house, he pulled on the laces of his hunting boots, wrapped them around the back, then the front, tugging them tight. He had on two wool shirts, along with an undershirt, and long johns under his jeans. His hunting knife was secured in the scabbard he wore on his thick leather belt.

The fireplace in the den crackled, logs shifted, sending sparks flying.

Dillon went over and added another log to the fire, knowing they would need the additional heat for the cold night. Without TV or radio and a reliable forecast, he could only guess how low the temperature would get. Maybe 25 degrees.

Holly was busy at the kitchen sink cutting vegetables by the waning afternoon light, saving the kerosene lamp for when it became dark. Rationing was a way of life.

"Holly, I'm heading out to go hunting."

"Be careful." She kissed him on the cheek. "How long will you be gone?"

"About two hours. Several times around dusk I've seen a big buck walking in the back pasture along the fence line near the branch. I'm guessing the water still left in the branch is attracting the buck. I need to get settled in the blind before the sun sets."

"Good luck," she said. "We could use fresh meat. I'll have something hot for you to eat when you come back. Cassie and Ryan promised to be back before dark so we can all eat together. Do you have everything you need?"

"I think so," Dillon said apprehensively. He thought about gearing up to take a Glock, but if he wasted any more time, he'd lose his window of opportunity.

Anytime Dillon suited up for a hunt, Buster paced the hardwood floor, his nails clicking and clattering. Standing eagerly at the door, Buster whined and wiggled from side to side anticipating the door to crack open so he could make an escape to go on the hunt. This time it was different, for it wasn't the hunt he was interested in.

Buster had studied Dillon's every move for the past hour and when Dillon's hand reached for the doorknob, Buster knew that was the signal the door was about to open.

"Sorry," Dillon said. He patted Buster on the head. "Not this time, boy."

With determined eyes, Buster squeezed closer to the door, mindful he was not being obedient. He rarely went against the wishes of his owner, but the dog sensed something wasn't right in the woods. The noises that the animals made at night foraging for food had been silent, and those that were active in the day stayed close to cover.

Birds flitted nervously from treetop to treetop. The scurrying animals quickened their steps, nervous eyes flicking to the dark shadows of the woods.

Hours earlier, Buster had accompanied Dillon while he chopped wood. Standing like a sentry, Buster had caught an unusual scent of deadly power and male domination carried by a fleeting wind current. His mind searched for the meaning. A long buried herding instinct to protect his pack came to Buster, and he had tried to nose Dillon away from the danger.

Dillon said, "Good dog! Wanna play?" Buster had only cocked his head in confusion because this was no time to play a game of 'fetch the stick' or bark like his owner encouraged him to.

Buster squeezed closer to the door.

"No," Dillon said, his tone forceful. He nudged the uncooperative dog away with a gentle push of his boot, making direct eye contact with Buster. "Leave!" With a quick movement, Dillon thrust out an arm, pointing his index finger at the corner of the room. Buster understood the command and the need to acquiesce to his owner's instructions.

Tucking his tail, Buster slunk away and padded over to his dog bed in the corner of the room. He scratched at his bedding then pillowed into it. His slack posture and sad eyes indicated he knew he would have to wait for his owner's return.

"What about the cats?" Dillon asked. "Is it too early to let them in?"

Holly put down the paring knife and walked over to where Dillon stood. "I'm worried about Tiger. I haven't seen him in a couple of days. If you see Princess let her in. She's been acting strange lately."

"I hope Tiger is okay," Dillon said. He had come to an understanding with Tiger, a gray and white stripped male tabby cat that was quickly becoming *his* cat. When nobody was looking, Dillon slipped Tiger an extra piece of meat and petted him on the head, saying "Good kitty." He had always considered himself a dog person, not a cat person. However, times were different now, and if anyone questioned his masculinity or the fact he liked cats, he'd tell them to go pound sand. Princess, a calico, was more Holly's cat, who meowed incessantly and liked to rub all over her legs.

On their way home from the unsuccessful trip to find Dillon's daughter, they had found the cats at the house, skinny, scrawny, and crying for food. Dillon had suggested shooting them and eating them to which Holly replied, "We aren't starving, they are." Ever since Holly had fed them that first night, the cats stayed.

"Come to think of it," Dillon said, "I haven't seen Tiger either."

"I can't quite put my finger on it," Holly said as she straightened Dillon's coat collar. "Princess is so skittish that any little noise sends her running."

Dillon shrugged. "I guess she's a…" he paused for effect, "…scaredy-cat?" He waited for Holly to roll her eyes. She didn't disappoint him.

"Not funny," Holly said.

"Sorry, I couldn't resist it. I'm sure Tiger is okay and probably went hunting for extra food."

"Probably." Holly wasn't convinced because it wasn't like Tiger to wander off for long. "See you in a bit." She shut the door behind him and glanced at Buster. Shaking her head, she huffed, "Men."

* * *

Walking along the hardened ruts of the dirt road leading to the back of the ranch, Dillon scanned the pastures and woods, searching for signs of the buck.

Due to the lack of rain, tracks were difficult to see in the ruddy soil. He was able to identify a raccoon track by the long fingers pressed into the dirt. A rabbit had passed by, and from the long stride of the prints, a coyote had been chasing it. Gauging from the size of the tracks and Dillon's limited knowledge, it had been a large one, though the track appeared different than a normal coyote.

Dillon squatted on his heels and studied the large print, tracing the outline with his hand.

Odd, he thought.

His mind went over different animals that could have left it. He chewed on the inside of his cheek and apprehensively checked his surroundings. Walking deeper into the ranch, the road drifted to the south before veering west toward the branch. While Dillon walked, he was mindful to keep to the undisturbed soil which softened his steps.

The sound of wings flapping caused him to take notice. A buzzard that had been sitting a few feet from the road lifted its head from the carrion, its eyes tracking the man walking on the road.

When Dillon breached that invisible line of no return, the buzzard clumsily flapped its wings to gather enough lift. The large bird flew awkwardly to a mid-sized tree where it sat perched on a branch, preening its feathers.

Deciding to inspect what type of carrion the buzzard was dining on, Dillon stepped off of the road and into high grass. It crunched under his boots.

Walking a few feet he stopped, his mind struggling to make sense of the gruesome scene.

The high grass had been tamped down, and stripped gray and white fur was scattered about, partially obscuring the bloody remnants of an animal skull. Bones had been picked clean and when Dillon pushed away the fur concentrated over the skull, he flinched and jumped back.

"Oh." He choked at the sight, and swallowed bile that had risen in his throat. The jaw with sharp, pointy teeth and whiskers could only mean one thing.

"Tiger," he said.

Dillon sighed heavily, letting his eyes roam over the land, for what he wasn't sure. "You poor cat. Ending up as coyote food."

He pondered how to tell Holly. She had such a soft heart for the cats and, Dillon hated to admit, so did he. Life was hard in the wilderness, especially for smaller animals. For a moment he thought about the food chain and how it wasn't any good to be on the bottom. Tiger hadn't stood a chance against the bigger predator. He swallowed the hard lump that had formed in his throat as sadness washed over him at the loss of his pet. As soon as he returned to the house, he'd have to tell Holly to keep Princess inside.

He'd come back later and bury what little bones and fur was left of Tiger.

Stepping away from the ghastly sight, Dillon resumed walking toward the natural blind. When he came to the tightly woven stand of saplings, vines, and bushes, he pushed through an opening and sat down on the canvas stool.

Scanning the open field, his eyes drifted eastward to the far end of the seasonal branch. A bitter chill was in the air announcing the coming long days of a cold winter.

Dillon tugged down his hunting cap.

Westward was the waning light, casting a pale gold upon the land. A gust of wind brushed the land and Dillon turned in the direction of the rustling leaves settling into a thick brown carpet along the slope of the branch.

He saw movement and lifted the rifle. It had only been the flash of a brilliant red male cardinal flitting through the bramble that had caught his eye, so he lowered the rifle.

Bundled in his coat, Dillon lifted an ear flap of his hunting cap, taking in the silent sounds of the woods. Even in the cold weather, animals foraged for food. An hour earlier, a nine banded armadillo skittered across a path and darted to its den, hidden by the roots of a massive oak.

Dillon sat so still a nervous rabbit hopped next to him, unaware of the statue of a man peering down at him. Amused by the twitchy rabbit, Dillon tapped his foot which sent the rabbit scurrying.

Time passed, the woods became eerily still.

Something strange was going on, because for the past thirty minutes there had been no animal movement. Even the comforting melodies of song birds had quieted.

Just a while longer, he thought.

Dillon had seen that big buck earlier in the week during one of his daily forays inspecting the five hundred acre ranch. He followed the tracks through underbrush and deadfalls and finally to the branch where he had lost the trail. Deer were creatures of habit, following old trails, keeping to the shadows and the cover of fall foliage. The buck had to be smart to live as long as this beauty did, walking the safe trails away from hunters.

Daylight waned in the late hour, gray clouds hanging low over the land. A crow glided across the darkening sky, cawing as it went. Another one joined in and Dillon tracked the pair landing in a faraway tree.

Movement at the branch!

Dillon swiveled his gaze, awed at the size of the buck.

With weighty trepidation the magnificent buck stepped out from the dark tree cover. It snorted and tossed its head covered with a full rack of antlers. Its tail switched nervously, showing the white fur. For a long moment it stood like a product of a skilled taxidermist, glassy eyes staring in Dillon's direction as if sensing another pair of eyes was watching it.

Satisfied there was no immediate danger, the deer stepped out to graze.

Dillon exhaled and slowly raised his .30-06 to where he had a clear shot. He peered through the sights, the crosshairs square on the deer. He put his index finger on the trigger, breathed out, ready for the shot.

The deer jerked its head up and glanced back to the shadows lining the branch. The tail swished faster, leg muscles rippled and the moment the deer understood the deadliness of the situation—that a predator lurked nearby—that moment it was about to leap, Dillon took the shot.

The rifle shot rent the silence of the woods, echoing along the contours of the branch.

The crows scattered, and a flock of doves roosting in an evergreen tree took flight, away from the crack of the rifle, away to safety.

The deer fell dead.

The shot had been perfect.

Dillon slung the rifle over his shoulder and emerged from the blind, his footfalls upon the land quick and purposeful.

Coming to the deer, he gazed at the beast prone on its side, a trickle of blood staining the tan hide. Dillon felt neither remorse nor satisfaction, only the knowledge their bellies would be full for the coming month.

He mulled over whether or not to field dress the deer where it fell. Considering the waning light and the fact he had not brought a lantern with him, he decided to drag it back to the house. Taking out a length of rope, he tied it to the antlers. Dragging it would be hard work, and he cursed himself for not stashing a wheelbarrow near the blind. Dragging the one hundred fifty pound buck was the best he could do.

Slinging the .30-06 over his shoulder, Dillon steeled himself, took the rope with both hands, and with a tremendous heave he moved the deer. Foot by agonizing foot, he struggled to drag the deer across the uneven terrain dotted with fire ant mounds and clumps of grass, and onto the ruts of the road, packed hard by countless trips of a ranch truck over the years.

Breathing hard, he stopped for a moment in the shadows of a large oak. He drew the back of his hand across his forehead where beads of sweat had formed. The sun slipped lower across the horizon, casting winter shadows across the land.

The woods were strangely silent.

The hair on the back of Dillon's neck prickled, sending a shiver throughout his body, and an intense foreboding captured him.

Shaking off the feeling, he pulled down on his hunting cap and adjusted the thick collar of his coat over his neck to ward off the chill. Taking the rope in both hands, he began to drag the deer again.

A powerful force knocked Dillon off his feet.

He was violently thrown to the ground, the air knocked out of him. His face mashed down into the weeds on the side of the road, and he struggled to catch his breath.

For a moment he thought a tree limb had slammed into his back, that was, until he heard growling and hissing.

Dillon's mind worked in overdrive trying to identify the animal.

Struggling to rise, he again was slammed to the ground, and this time, a biting pressure clamped down on the back of his neck. The pressure increased, yet Dillon felt no pain.

He clawed and struck at the attacker, his hands brushing against short, wiry hair. Somehow he managed to turn his head, catching a glimpse of the beast.

Amber eyes rimmed in black locked on his, the ears were flat against its tawny head, and the beast opened its mouth into a snarl, showing its teeth.

It was a mountain lion, and it was massive!

When Dillon tried to rise the lion jumped on him again and sunk sharp teeth meant for grinding and slashing into the collar of his thick jacket.

Dillon was pinned face down.

It was a fight to the death. With wild abandon, the mountain lion slashed and bit into Dillon's thick winter coat.

The .30-06 had been knocked away, out of Dillon's grasp. His Glock had been left at the house.

Think!

The knife!

Dillon struggled to release his hunting knife from the scabbard, but with the powerful animal pinning him down, he couldn't get to it.

Think!

His assisted-opening razor sharp Kershaw knife with a three and a half inch blade was in his back pocket. He reached around, pulled it out, and flipped it open.

For a brief second the animal halted its attack.

Dillon heaved his body over to where he was facing the mountain lion head on.

He brought up his Kershaw.

The lion opened its mouth wide and lunged.

Dillon made a defensive move with his left arm which the lion sunk his teeth into.

With the mountain lion's neck exposed, Dillon thrust the knife into the soft part of the neck where he thought the carotid artery would be.

The lion screamed, yet it refused to relinquish the hold it had on its prey.

Dillon pushed harder and sliced backward, opening the neck.

Blood gushed out of the lion's neck and onto Dillon, staining his jacket in crimson.

Dillon held the knife steady, the blade still thrust deep into the lion's neck.

Seconds ticked by which seemed like hours. The lion panted and its grip on Dillon's left arm loosened. Legs and claws slashed listlessly.

The lion's strength waned as sure as the sun was setting, and as the sun slid further beneath the horizon, the lion gasped one last time for air then fell silent.

A buzzard sitting high in a nearby tree watched the attack with vague curiosity. Turning its head, it casually resumed preening itself.

Dillon pushed the dead mountain lion off of him. Stunned and with adrenaline still rushing through him, he laid back down on the cold ground. He concentrated on breathing to calm his racing heart.

Breathe.

He felt around his neck checking for puncture wounds, and miraculously, there were none. His collar was all torn up and shredded, and no telling what had happened to his hunting cap. He did have a nasty scratch on his neck, but with a good cleaning and antibiotic ointment, it would heal.

His thick coat now covered in blood had saved him from a slashing by the lion.

Dillon moved his arms and legs, and flexed his fingers, testing them for injuries or broken bones.

Somehow, he had come out mortally unscathed.

The odd happenings of the past few days now made sense: the horses pacing restlessly, Tiger missing, Princess acting odd, the hair on his neck standing up, lack of animal activity, and even Buster acting protective.

Dillon wasn't sure how long he lay on the ground. Maybe five minutes, maybe ten. However long it had been, the night had become darker, and without any ambient light from the moon or stars, Dillon got on his hands and knees and crawled around, searching for his rifle. Finding it, he kept it near as he went about the process of rigging up the rope to the deer so he could drag it back home.

From his knowledge of mountain lions they were solitary animals only until it was mating season. And with spring a few months away, a female lion could be near. He would need to be vigilant whenever outside because a hungry mountain lion with cubs would kill about anything.

Dillon's eyes flicked to the mountain lion, studying it to make sure it was dead. In life it was a magnificent beast, in death, nothing.

It had been a massive animal in the prime of its life, obviously healthy with a thick coat, possibly weighing close to what Dillon weighed. He bent down on one knee and tentatively lifted one of the lion's lips, still warm and supple. The teeth were sharp and unbroken, gums healthy.

Rising, Dillon stood there a moment and ran his hands over his stubbly beard, thinking.

He was going to drag that son of a bitch home come hell or high water, because that lion would make one mighty fine rug.

The End

About the Author

Chris Pike grew up in the woodlands of Central Texas and along the Texas Gulf Coast, fishing, hunting, hiking, camping, and dodging hurricanes and tropical storms. Chris has learned that the power of Mother Nature is daunting from sizzling temperatures or icy conditions; from drought to category five hurricanes. Living without electricity for two weeks in the sweltering August heat after Hurricane Ike proved to be challenging. It paid to be prepared.

Currently living in Houston, Texas, Chris is married, has two grown daughters, one dog, and three overweight, demanding cats.

Chris is an avid supporter of the Second Amendment, and has held a Texas concealed carry permit since 1998, with the Glock being the current gun of choice. Chris is a graduate of the University of Texas and has a BBA in Marketing. By day Chris works as a database manager for a large international company, while by night an Indie author.

Got a question or a comment? Email Chris at Chris.Pike123@aol.com. Your email will be answered promptly and your address will never be shared with anyone.

Unknown World
Book 3

Chris is currently working on Unknown World which will be a standalone book based on characters introduced in Book 2. Stay tuned for the story of Chris Chandler and Amanda Hardy as they encounter dangerous obstacles on their way to Austin. A 2017 publication date is planned. A sneak peek is available, so email Chris if you'd like to sample it. In keeping with the animals the main character of each book has to fight off, Chandler will also have to fight a deadly wild animal, one that lurks in the shadows of Texas woodlands. Want to know what it is? Write Chris at Chris.Pike123@aol.com to find out.

Next in the series will be the story of Garrett, who was also introduced in Book 2. Garrett is a natural leader and people will look to him for guidance in the new world.

Also, an epic sci-fi series has been rattling around in Chris's head for years, so hopefully that story will come to fruition sometime in late 2017 or early 2018.

Before You Go…

One last thing. Thank you, thank you, thank you for downloading this book. Without the support of readers like yourself, Indie publishing would not be possible.

I've heard from a lot of my readers, and for those who have written me, you know I always answer your emails. You have taught me a lot with your expertise in electronics, medicine, and basically how things work which is especially needed for your mechanically challenged author. Your encouragement has inspired me to keep writing. Thank you.

Another way to show your support of an Indie author is to write an honest review on Amazon. It helps other readers make a decision to download the book. A few words or one sentence is all it takes.

So please consider writing a review. I will be forever grateful.

Also, this book has been edited, proofed, and proofed again, but mistakes or typos are bound to happen. If you find a mistake, email me at Chris.Pike123@aol.com and it will be corrected.

All the best,
Chris

Made in the USA
Middletown, DE
05 December 2016